"Helping

It was like a slap in the face, wrapping her arms around herself, Paige shrugged. "If that's how you feel, forget I offered."

"I will." He turned the doorknob and jerked the door open.

"Do you think the only person you're hurting is yourself?" she asked, keeping her voice low.

"I'm not hurting you, that's for sure."

"You're hurting your family. Don't you care?"

"I hardly know my family." His voice was bitter, but he made the mistake of glancing at her, and his eyes betrayed him.

He'd taken one step out the door when she spoke. "And what about your son?"

The question stopped him in his tracks. Turning back, his cold gaze met hers. "Thanks for the prescription."

Before she could say anything else, he was out of the room, and she watched him walk down the hallway to the waiting room. She'd heard war was hell, and Tucker O'Brien was living proof of it.

Dear Reader,

I've received many emails and notes from readers asking if Tucker O'Brien will ever have his own story. As you can see, he does, and it's a joy to finally hold Tucker's story in my hands. The idea of the O'Brien family—brothers Tucker and Tanner—isn't all that new and was originally conceived over ten years ago. But the time never seemed right for them, until the town and people of Desperation took root in my mind and my heart.

Tucker was first introduced to readers in *The Rodeo Rider*, released in 2009 and the beginning of the stories set in Desperation, Oklahoma. Even then, I wasn't quite sure who Tucker was, where he was or even where he had been. Not until he walked into Nikki and Mac's wedding reception in *The Reluctant Wrangler*, limping and using a cane, did I have an inkling of who he had become. His pain is not only physical, but emotional, and it will take Dr. Paige Miles, a woman who has dedicated her life to helping others, to break through the wall that Tucker has built around himself.

I hope readers will enjoy *The Maverick's Reward*, as Tucker and Paige learn about each other, themselves... and about love.

Best wishes and happy reading!

Roxann

The Maverick's Reward

ROXANN DELANEY

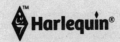

Harlequin®

TORONTO NEW YORK LONDON
AMSTERDAM PARIS SYDNEY HAMBURG
STOCKHOLM ATHENS TOKYO MILAN MADRID
PRAGUE WARSAW BUDAPEST AUCKLAND

If you purchased this book without a cover you should be aware that this book is stolen property. It was reported as "unsold and destroyed" to the publisher, and neither the author nor the publisher has received any payment for this "stripped book."

Recycling programs
for this product may
not exist in your area.

ISBN-13: 978-0-373-75361-1

THE MAVERICK'S REWARD

Copyright © 2011 by Roxann Farmer

All rights reserved. Except for use in any review, the reproduction or utilization of this work in whole or in part in any form by any electronic, mechanical or other means, now known or hereafter invented, including xerography, photocopying and recording, or in any information storage or retrieval system, is forbidden without the written permission of the publisher, Harlequin Enterprises Limited, 225 Duncan Mill Road, Don Mills, Ontario M3B 3K9, Canada.

This is a work of fiction. Names, characters, places and incidents are either the product of the author's imagination or are used fictitiously, and any resemblance to actual persons, living or dead, business establishments, events or locales is entirely coincidental.

This edition published by arrangement with Harlequin Books S.A.

For questions and comments about the quality of this book please contact us at Customer_eCare@Harlequin.ca

® and TM are trademarks of the publisher. Trademarks indicated with ® are registered in the United States Patent and Trademark Office, the Canadian Trade Marks Office and in other countries.

www.Harlequin.com

Printed in U.S.A.

ABOUT THE AUTHOR

Roxann Delaney doesn't remember a time when she wasn't reading or writing, and she always loved that touch of romance in both. A native Kansan, she's lived on a farm, in a small town and has returned to live in the city where she was born. Her four daughters and grandchildren keep her busy when she isn't writing or designing websites. The 1999 Maggie award winner is excited to be a part of the Harlequin American Romance line and loves to hear from readers. Contact her at roxann@roxanndelaney.com or visit her website www.roxanndelaney.com.

Books by Roxann Delaney

HARLEQUIN AMERICAN ROMANCE

1194—FAMILY BY DESIGN
1269—THE RODEO RIDER
1292—BACHELOR COWBOY
1313—THE LAWMAN'S LITTLE SURPRISE
1327—THE RELUCTANT WRANGLER

Don't miss any of our special offers. Write to us at the following address for information on our newest releases.

Harlequin Reader Service
U.S.: 3010 Walden Ave., P.O. Box 1325, Buffalo, NY 14269
Canadian: P.O. Box 609, Fort Erie, Ont. L2A 5X3

In memory of
SP4 Patrick Elvin McCullough, 1949–1969.

Heartfelt thanks to our veterans for their service and
to the families and friends who've lost loved ones.

Chapter One

Pain shot up his leg and knee, radiating into every inch of his body, but Tucker O'Brien worked through it as the nurse stepped out of the examining room. He hadn't planned to be in the small doctor's office in Desperation, Oklahoma, but nothing was going as he'd thought it would.

When the pain subsided, he relaxed as much as he could. It would return, but for now he could breathe more easily. He glanced around the room, noting that it was nothing out of the ordinary and much the same as he remembered as a boy. The old doctor, Doc Priller, had stitched and bandaged him many times, more often than not because he'd refused to stay off the back of any animal that would hold still long enough for him to climb onto it. He managed a small smile, but was immediately hit by another wave of pain and barely noticed the door open when he heard someone speak.

"Fran tells me you're looking for some pain meds."

Steeling himself against the onslaught his body was enduring, Tucker nodded. As the pain began to abate, one thought became clear in his mind. Everybody had talked about Dr. Page, but nobody had mentioned she was a woman. There must have been a mistake when he'd made the appointment.

She held out her hand, which he took with reluctance, and introduced herself. "I'm Dr. Miles."

So there *had* been a mistake, and he was more than willing to correct it. "Tucker O'Brien," he grudgingly answered. "But I'm here to see Dr. Page."

For a moment, she didn't answer, then a smile broke out on her face and she laughed softly as she pulled her hand away. "Maybe I should have said I'm Dr. Paige Miles. Does that clear it up?"

He answered with a brief nod. It cleared it up, all right, but it didn't make this visit any easier. Why hadn't someone told him?

She took a seat on a small metal stool and opened a file folder. "Now that we have that straightened out, why aren't you at the VA?" she asked as she read through his file.

With the pain on its way to bearable, he felt able to answer. "Because it's too bad to drive that far."

"The pain is too bad? Then how did you get here?"

Sizing up the doctor immediately, he suspected that any answer he gave wouldn't help the situation, so he remained silent.

She closed the folder and placed it on her lap. "I'm sure any of the O'Briens would be happy to drive you, if you told them why."

"I don't want to bother them." His brother, Tanner, least of all.

Her brown hair was pulled back in a knot, and she tilted her head to the side, studying him. "Why do you think they'd be bothered?"

He didn't like her questions. His relationship with his

family wasn't her business. He didn't need to answer personal questions, and if that's what she was going to ask, he'd go somewhere else. Getting to his feet, he stood straight and reached for his cane.

"Are you leaving?" she asked, sitting perfectly still, her hands folded on top of the folder.

"I've already seen a shrink. I came for some pain pills. If you aren't going to give me a prescription, then I'm wasting my time and yours."

He hadn't taken two steps when she spoke again. "I didn't say I wouldn't."

Her large brown eyes made him think of sweet chocolate, but he brushed the thought aside. This wasn't the time for that sort of thing. If there ever was a time. "You didn't say you would," he pointed out.

Leaning back against the cabinet behind her, she crossed her legs and stared at him.

He focused on her legs.

"I'm simply trying to determine why you aren't on your way to Oklahoma City to the VA hospital," she explained.

"I told you why."

"Have you had a prescription written by a doctor there?"

He hadn't expected this to be so difficult. But now that he was here, it figured the woman would give him trouble. "When I was a patient, yes."

She opened the folder again and studied it. "When were you released?" she asked and looked up at him.

"I—" He had a feeling that if he told her the truth— that he hadn't been released, he'd just walked out—she'd give him hell. "Does it matter?"

She motioned for him to return to the examining

table. "I'm not familiar with your case," she said, when he'd settled back on the table. "I need to know when you've last seen your doctor, if your condition is improving or not and what medications you're taking." When he didn't answer, she added, "It's my job to find out these things so I can help you."

He nodded, but he wasn't happy. Luckily, the pain seemed to have subsided. "Six weeks ago on the doctor visit. My condition isn't expected to improve. And I was on anxiety and pain meds until recently." It was the last part he hated the most.

"I see. How recently?"

"Not since I left the hospital."

"And you weren't given a prescription at that time?"

She was going to dig until he told her every last detail, so he might as well get down to the bottom line. "I was never released, and I thought I could go without the meds."

"Why?"

"Because I don't like taking them."

"But they obviously help the pain or you wouldn't be here."

Hating that he'd failed at his attempt to rid himself of the drugs he'd relied on for most of the year, he wasn't all that willing to explain. He'd thought he could handle the pain. He'd thought wrong. "Apparently they do, so if you'll just write a prescription—"

"I'll have to call your doctor at the VA first."

Tucker didn't care if she called the president of the United States for permission. He needed the meds, whether he wanted them or not. "So call him."

She was quiet for a moment, watching him, and then she stood. "It won't take long."

Before he could think of a reply, she was out the door. He began to wonder why she hadn't asked about his leg. Not that he would have told her much, but he suspected she might know some of his history from his family. By now, most everyone probably knew about the eight months he had spent as a prisoner in Somalia.

He'd screwed up. There was no denying it. The Special Forces rescue mission he'd been involved in had gone wrong, although the aid workers were rescued. But he and another marine had been captured by rebels in the process. Their injuries hadn't been treated. Somehow he'd managed to hold on until he was found and returned to the States early last fall with a leg that would probably never work right. Because of that, his brain was turning to mush on pain pills. Smithson hadn't been so lucky. Smithson didn't last three months. Just who was the lucky one?

And now he had this doctor who couldn't seem to write a damn prescription without help. Coming back to Desperation last month had been the worst decision he'd made since he'd left nineteen years ago.

PAIGE TUCKED THE PHONE against her shoulder as she listened to the Veteran's Administration doctor who had treated Tucker O'Brien give her the details of the case. "I'll make sure he's monitored," she said, jotting notes in the file on her desk. "I wasn't aware of the extent of his injuries or the surgery, but now that I know…"

She listened to what Dr. Fuller was telling her, but her mind was trying to wrap itself around what the patient had endured. It was no wonder he was so belligerent. She was amazed he was even alive.

"I'll give him another month of meds and await the file you have on him," she said when the doctor had finished. "But I might as well tell you, I don't think he'll continue to be my patient. I'll keep an eye on him, anyway. I know his family."

"I wouldn't count on him coming back here to the VA," the doctor said. "He never should have left the hospital when he did, but there was no stopping him."

Paige didn't doubt it. From the little she had seen of what might be her newest patient, he didn't appear to be a person who did things the way they should be done. But no matter what his story was, she was still a doctor and was only interested in his health, not making him happy.

After thanking the VA doctor, she hung up the phone and stared at it. She knew Tucker O'Brien had recently returned home from the service, followed by treatment in a veteran's hospital, but she hadn't known any details or how many hospitals. The O'Briens didn't talk about it, at least not to anyone outside the family, and it hadn't been any of her business to ask. Until now. She wondered, too, just how much *they* knew about what had happened in Somalia. Considering Tucker's lack of communication with her, she doubted he'd told them anything.

Pushing away from her desk, she stood, massaging her temples with her fingers. She loved practicing in Desperation, but some days were more stressful than others. She was thankful it was Friday and hoped there wouldn't be any emergencies she would need to tend to over the weekend.

After reaching for a prescription pad in her drawer, she wrote a new script for Tucker and headed back to the examining room, hoping he hadn't skipped out on her.

When she walked into the room, he looked up at her, his deep brown eyes taking her breath away. "That long to get an okay on meds?" he asked, his voice filled with distrust and a hint of pain.

"They had to hunt down Dr. Fuller," she explained and handed him the prescription.

He took it from her and stuffed it in his pocket. "Thanks."

The word contained no gratitude, but she ignored it. There were more important issues to discuss. "Do you understand how dangerous it is to simply stop taking certain drugs?"

"I didn't just stop taking them."

"You weaned yourself off the pain medication?" When he nodded, she had to know. "In the hospital?"

"It isn't that hard."

She could only guess at how he'd done it. "It should be done under supervision," she told him. But he obviously did things his own way, on his own terms. There was no doubt he needed the pain meds. Even now she could see it in his eyes as he stepped down from the table.

"I'll need to see you again in a week or two," she told him as he started for the door.

He stopped as he reached for the doorknob, and his back stiffened. "Maybe I'll just go back to the VA."

"You go wherever you think is best for you. But if going from doctor to doctor is what you have in mind, let me warn you that you'll get nothing but heartache, if not worse, when all is said and done."

He turned to look at her, and his eyes narrowed. "Worse? Lady, I've already seen worse."

She couldn't respond to that, knowing at least some of what he'd been through, so she simply inclined her head to show she understood. Still, she had a point to make and a patient to care for. "Drug addiction isn't pretty."

"I'm not an addict," he said, his voice raised. "I was trying to get *off* the stuff, not take more."

"But it's obvious you can't do that." She watched him lower his head and knew she'd hit at what bothered him. But she wasn't finished. "Yet," she added.

His head jerked up, and he stared at her, doubt in his eyes. "What do you mean by that?"

Turning away from him, she laid his file on the counter. "There are other ways."

"To take care of *this?*"

She didn't need to see him to know he was referring to a leg she was certain was weak and might soon be worthless. But that was his fault and no one else's.

When she turned around to face him again, she saw not only his disbelief, but also his sorrow. "Yes, to take care of *that*," she answered, trying hard not to show how much his pain bothered her.

"Like what?"

Not quite ready to give him details, she tried for a smile. "Let's talk about it in a week or so. If you'll come back, that is."

His internal struggle was clear. "I had the surgery."

"What about physical therapy?"

"It didn't do any good, except to get me on my feet."

According to Dr. Fuller, Tucker hadn't bothered with much after that. He'd simply packed his things and left the hospital, barely able to manage walking. Now that she'd met him, she wasn't surprised. It didn't help that some veteran's hospitals were understaffed. Too many men and women from all branches of the service were coming home every day and sometimes not getting the care they needed. Especially the ones like Tucker.

Someone needed to step in and set things right with him, and it appeared that, at least for now, she was the one. "How long has it been since you've done any physical therapy and what kind?" She already knew the answer, but she wanted to see if he could be honest.

"I don't know what kind."

"How long ago?"

He hesitated before answering. "Months."

Because she hated to push him, she hesitated to ask more. Perhaps Dr. Fuller would send that information, but if she wanted to help Tucker—which she did—she needed the information so she would know where to start.

"How many months?" she asked. When he didn't immediately answer, she pushed. "More than six?"

He shook his head, but said nothing.

Even that wasn't good news. If, as Dr. Fuller had briefly touched on, Tucker had had muscle or nerve injuries with the unattended multiple breaks in his leg, and in spite of reconstructive surgery, the lack of therapy would make matters worse. And then there was the ACL surgery. It also depended on something else. "When did you start therapy?"

He shook his head. "I don't remember. After the surgery at—" He stopped and took a breath, avoiding even a glance at her directly. "In Tampa, first. They had me pretty doped up. I don't remember much. Then some in Muskogee, and then with Dr. Fuller."

What worried her was that he had given up on the therapy. But even more, she worried about his mental state. She knew what giving up did to a patient. She'd experienced the worst, and she didn't want Tucker or the O'Briens to go through anything like that. They'd gone through enough already, from what she'd heard. And Tucker had endured even more. She couldn't make him do something he refused to do, any more than she'd been able to make Jeff keep up with *his* therapy.

It had been years since she'd thought of the young man who'd been a patient during her internship, and remembering it now made her all that more determined to do whatever it took to keep Tucker from what had happened to Jeff.

She took a deep breath, certain he would rebuke her for her effort, but she had to try. "Are you willing to give therapy a try again?"

That got his attention. "Why?"

"Why do you think? Do you understand that without it, you could lose the use of your leg?" Memories swamped her, only making her more determined to help him.

"I'm not going back to the VA."

"The VA isn't the only place."

"There aren't any physical therapists in Desperation, so how do you propose I go about it?"

"I'll check around, if you'll agree to see it through."

His laugh was cold and without humor. "Considering

how packed that waiting room was, I'm sure you have all the time in the world."

His sarcasm stung, but she ignored it. "I have some free time."

He was silent for a moment while he stared at her. "Helping out a cripple, huh?"

It was like a slap in the face, but instead of wrapping her arms around herself, she shrugged. "If that's how you feel, forget I offered."

"I will." He turned the doorknob and jerked the door open.

"Do you think the only person you're hurting is yourself?" she asked, keeping her voice low.

"I'm not hurting you, that's for sure."

"You're hurting your family. Don't you care?"

"I hardly know my family." There was bitterness in his voice, but he made the mistake of glancing at her, and his eyes betrayed him.

He'd taken one step out the door when she spoke. "And what about your son?"

The question stopped him in his tracks. Turning back, his cold gaze met hers. "Thanks for the prescription."

Before she could say anything else, he was out of the room, and she watched him walk down the hallway to the waiting room. She'd heard war was hell, and Tucker O'Brien was living proof of it.

"Did you see the doctor?" Jules O'Brien asked as she set the table on the patio for dinner.

Tucker had been trying to think of how he could help, but his sister-in-law's question left him staring at her. Nobody could read him so well, except for his sister,

Nikki, and he barely knew either of them. "Yeah, I saw her. How did you know I was going to?"

Jules shrugged and concentrated on laying the plates on the table. "You asked about her once or twice." She looked up at him with a sly smile. "And you left a paper with a date and time on the kitchen counter one morning, next to the open phone book."

"And here I thought you were some kind of great detective," he said, hoping to keep the conversation light. He'd rather there was no conversation, but it hadn't taken him long to understand that Jules was always looking for a way to include him in everything, even conversation.

"Being observant is part of being a psychologist." She flashed him a smile. "I can't help myself."

He nodded, but said nothing. He'd told his family only a little about his injuries and the eight months he'd spent in the tiny, primitive prison in Somalia, but it had been enough for Jules to put two and two together without asking questions.

"So what did you think of our doctor?" she asked.

Thankful that he could pull his thoughts from a past he wanted to forget, he considered her question and how he should answer it. Should he mention that he hadn't expected a woman doctor? Or one so young and pretty? Jules would probably make something of that, so he decided to avoid that one. "She's all right."

"Trish and Kate raved about her, and even Rowdy has been impressed."

He had to do some thinking to remember who all these people were. Rowdy, he knew from his childhood. The O'Briens' Rocking O Ranch foreman had been like a surrogate father after Tucker's dad was killed while bull riding. But Tucker hadn't stuck around for long after that. Four years later, he was traveling the rodeo circuit on his own. It had been a foolish decision, but he couldn't change the mistakes of his past.

Once again he had to force his mind from the past and focus on what he needed to remember. Trish was Trish Rule, wife of the local sheriff and the sister of Kate McPherson, who was the wife of his brother's partner in a rodeo stock company. Jules and Tanner talked about the families often. Too often, as far as he was concerned.

Jules stood on the opposite side of the table, watching him. "But you did like the doctor?"

Unwilling to say exactly what he thought about Dr. Miles, he shrugged his shoulders. The truth was he thought the good doctor, in spite of how pretty she was, had a lot of gall asking him so many questions and acting like he was some kind of addict. He wasn't yet ready to admit that she was doing everything she was supposed to. He wasn't too fond of anyone in the medical profession. Experience told him they couldn't help him, so what did it matter?

"Looks like there's going to be a crowd," he said, when she placed the last of the plates and glasses on the table.

"Ten of us, not counting the little ones."

Ten? Who the hell was going to be there?

But he knew that wasn't fair. It wasn't his home, although he had grown up and lived there until he was fifteen. He didn't have any right to question who she and Tanner invited to dinner. If it had been up to him, he would have skipped it, but both of them, along with others, hadn't given him the chance. They expected him to be a part of the family.

His sister and their Cherokee grandmother were the only family he'd seen after leaving home. His grandmother had helped him make his way to the Marine Corps. After arriving at the VA in Oklahoma City a few months ago, he'd called her to let her know he was alive. She'd been the one who told him he'd fathered a child, almost nineteen years ago. The news had gotten him on his feet and on the way home. He'd seen his sister when he'd visited their grandmother, all those years ago, although they'd never spoken. Somehow she'd remembered him and had been the first to recognize him when he arrived at her wedding reception, nearly three weeks ago.

"I haven't heard from Nikki lately," he said. "Will she and Mac be here?"

"No, but I expect to hear from them soon." Jules moved toward the house. "Even though they're touring as many equine assisted psychotherapy programs and ranches as they can—" She stopped and chuckled. "Nikki is thirsty for knowledge, but I doubt she wants to be away from Kirby and the other boys very long."

Nodding as if he understood, Tucker waited until she'd gone into the house, and then he leaned heavily on his cane. The pain meds he was taking again, thanks to the doctor, did the job they were supposed to, but they left him weak. Not just his leg, which he'd accepted would never be normal again, but all of him. For someone who was a special ops marine, weakness was almost worse than pain. He'd rather not have either, but he hadn't been given a choice.

Not knowing where he would be sitting at the table

when the time came to eat and unable to carry much of anything with one free hand, he leaned against the rough bark of a nearby tree and waited. He didn't mind the solitude. In fact, he welcomed it. After spending months in hospital with nurses and doctors poking at him constantly, and the early barrage of questions from his family immediately after he returned to the Rocking O Ranch, being alone, if only for a few minutes, was a relief.

It wasn't long before he heard voices, and he pushed away from the tree just as Jules returned. Her hands were full of dishes of delicious-smelling food, and she was followed by a woman with long auburn hair, who held a baby.

"Go ahead and sit down," Jules told him, nodding toward the chair at the end of the table. "You know Kate, don't you?"

He turned his head toward the woman and nodded in greeting, remembering she was Tanner's partner's wife.

"It's good to see you again, Tucker," the woman said with a pleasant smile. "I hope you're enjoying your family as much as they're enjoying having you here."

"Thanks," he replied, hoping that would end the conversation.

Shifting the sleeping child in her arms, she turned to Jules. "I didn't see Wyoming."

"Tanner is bringing him down. More than likely, he's giving his daddy trouble," Jules answered, laughing.

At least Tucker knew that Wyoming was Jules and Tanner's two-year-old son. The rest? Only time would solve the problem of keeping everyone straight.

"If you'll tell me where I can put Tyler and Travis,"

the redhead was saying, "I'll have Dusty put up the playpens and baby monitor so I can help you with the food."

"I was thinking the family room would be perfect," Jules said, bustling around the table. "We'll be able to see them and, with the monitor, hear every little whimper, if there should be any."

Kate laughed, and then immediately quieted as she glanced at the baby. "Have no fear. Once Travis wakes up, we could hear him from the barn, without the monitor."

The women laughed softly together as they left the room, and once they were gone, Tucker pulled out the chair Jules had indicated and settled onto it. He felt out of place at the table and would have preferred being anywhere else. But he wouldn't beg off on attending this little get-together. He wouldn't do that to Jules. She somehow always managed to make him feel welcome without questions. He appreciated that. At least his brother had found a good woman.

"Here, let me take that."

Tucker looked up to see a dark-haired man with his hand extended, and he realized the man was offering to dispose of his cane. "Thanks. Sometimes it's a nuisance."

When the cane was leaning against the tree and out of the way, the man gave him a smile. "Morgan Rule," he said, introducing himself.

"Desperation's sheriff," Tucker replied with a nod and tried to smile.

Morgan shrugged. "It keeps me out of trouble. Anything I can get you?" When Tucker stiffened, the sheriff settled on a nearby chair. "I may not have been in the service, but I was a police officer in Miami for a time. There are places there that sometimes resemble a war zone."

"I've heard it's rough in some spots."

"My partner was killed in a drive-by shooting, if that gives you an idea of how bad it can get. I came here six months later."

"There's a little bit of hell everywhere," Tucker said, keeping his voice low, as others began to wander into the dining room.

He'd always found it easier to talk with someone who understood, even if they hadn't served in the armed forces. Morgan's understanding of the kinds of hell in the world and the insanity it caused made him feel less isolated.

Family and friends began to gather in the room, and Jules directed them to their seats. When he felt someone press a hand on his shoulder, he looked up to see his Aunt Bridey and offered what he hoped was a smile.

"I'm glad you decided to join us," she whispered, before moving on to the other side of the table at the opposite end.

He'd never planned to return to the ranch, until he'd learned he had a son. When he arrived, Jules and Tanner had insisted he stay. He hadn't felt he had a choice when he learned Shawn would be graduating from high school in two months. There wouldn't be a lot of time for them to get to know each other, especially with Shawn's plans to be gone for the summer, before college in the fall. Tucker wanted to be able to say each day was getting easier with his family, but he couldn't honestly say it was, even though some were better than others.

His heart soared with pride when Shawn came out of

the house to join them, laughing and joking with Kate, but he also felt the shame that snaked its way through him at the thought of not knowing he'd fathered a child. At least he'd returned in time to get to know his son, if only he knew how to do that.

"Wonderful! I was afraid you weren't going to make it," he heard Jules say from behind him.

"Nothing could have kept me away," a woman answered.

Tucker didn't have any trouble recognizing the voice of Desperation's new doctor. And he wasn't especially happy that she was joining them.

Chapter Two

"You've met Tucker," Jules said as she indicated the chair between Tucker and Morgan Rule. "And Morgan, too."

"Yes," Paige answered, smiling at Desperation's sheriff and giving a brief nod to Tucker. It wouldn't do any good to smile at him. He'd probably growl at her.

As soon as the thought entered her mind, she ducked her head, ashamed that she'd allowed her emotions to rule. He had more than enough to deal with, considering the pain his leg probably caused him. But he wouldn't be getting rid of that pain if he didn't get the therapy he needed. She feared he wouldn't.

Needing to put aside her concern for someone who didn't welcome it, she took her seat at the table and turned to the man on her right. "How's Krista getting along, Morgan?"

His smile was wry as he shook his head and chuckled. "All she wants to do is stand. I think the only time she doesn't is when she sleeps or Trish feeds her in the high chair."

"She's how old now?" Paige asked, quickly calculating. "Eight months? Is she cruising the furniture?

Hanging on to it as she walks?" When he nodded, she smiled. "She'll be walking on her own, in no time."

Morgan laughed. "And then nothing will be safe."

Trish, Morgan's wife, was sitting on the other side of him and leaned forward. "We're so glad you could join us, Paige. I know how busy you are."

"It was nice of Jules to invite me," Paige answered, always happy to spend time with Jules and her friends. If only Jules hadn't put her next to Tucker, she wouldn't feel so uncomfortable.

"Hey, Uncle Tanner, did you hear?" Shawn asked from the other side of the table. "Dusty's going to help Kate with the food for senior class night."

"Is that so?" Tanner replied, looking down the length of the table at his business partner.

"Kate is going to make her barbecue sandwiches," Shawn continued, "like she always does, but this year Dusty's smoking a turkey, too."

"In a smoker," Dusty said, "not rolled up like a cigar."

Kate passed a plate piled high with corn-on-the-cob. "He's getting good with that smoker."

Beside her, Dusty took the plate from her. "When you're married to the best cook in the county, it looks bad if you can't make a decent sandwich. Never thought I'd enjoy cooking, but that smoker has me hunting for new recipes."

"Where's the party being held?" Paige asked.

Shawn looked at Jules and grinned. "Uncle Tanner said we could have it in the workshop building. Some of us are making a list of things we need to do to get it ready."

Morgan held the platter of grilled steaks for Paige as

he spoke to everyone. "I heard Hettie agreed to allow the school to use the big barn at the Commune for the prom," he said.

"Shawn talked her into it," Trish explained. "Or at least that's what Hettie told Aunt Aggie."

Hettie Lambert and Aggie Clayborne were both Paige's patients and lifelong residents of Desperation. Hettie had given over her family home for use as the Shadydrive Retirement Home, commonly referred to as the Commune. As for Aggie, Trish and Kate's aunt, most everyone knew that wherever Hettie went, Aggie was close behind.

"It was Hettie who talked the school board into agreeing to it," Shawn explained. "Having it at the high school wasn't going to work out, and we wanted someplace different."

"What about the after-prom party?" Jules asked.

"It'll be there, too," Shawn answered. "And Ernie volunteered Freda to cook breakfast."

Paige listened as the conversation at the table continued. She'd been approached to act as chaperone at the prom and knew Tanner and Jules had been, too, along with others she knew, including Ernie Dolan, who managed the Commune, and Freda, his cook there. Hearing about the people who'd become her patients and others in Desperation was enjoyable. The stories and chitchat always made her feel closer to the community.

Before she knew it, dinner was over, and when Jules started to clear the table, Paige jumped up to help. She followed her into the big kitchen, where Bridey stood at the sink, rinsing the serving dishes.

"All three babies are sleeping," Kate announced with a big smile as she walked into the kitchen.

Trish, right behind her, sighed. "All of them at the same time. It's a miracle."

Working together, cleanup went quickly. With the warm afternoon awaiting them, Jules suggested they return to the patio and join the men. As expected, the talk of sports came to a stop when the women stepped out onto the flagstone. Once again, Paige found herself seated next to Tucker, but this time, she was determined to be sociable.

"How are those pain pills working?" she asked him, keeping her voice low.

"Fine."

Unwilling to let him shut her out, she continued. "Have you given any more thought to my suggestion?"

"What suggestion is that?" He turned slowly to look at her. "Oh, the PT. Sure, a little. It isn't for me."

She wasn't going to let him do this to himself. She was a doctor, and allowing a person to harm himself wasn't something she could do. "I'm sorry you believe that."

"Are you?"

"What is it that gave you this distrust of doctors?" she asked, stinging from the sarcasm in his voice.

As he stared straight ahead, a muscle in his jaw jumped.

"I wish you'd give it some thought," she urged. When it appeared he had a curt reply at the ready, she hurried on. "Oh, I know, you did, but try it again."

He turned his gaze on her. "Why would I do that?"

"Because I really believe it can help you."

"You're putting your faith in the wrong man."

Before she could think of a response, he'd grabbed his cane and was struggling to his feet. It took every bit of resolve she had not to move to help him. Instead, she remained seated and focused her attention on the others, who were in a heated discussion about the latest college baseball game.

But she couldn't stop the feeling of helplessness that came over her. Somehow she would find a way to reach Tucker before things became worse.

TUCKER MADE HIS WAY slowly into the house, glad to get away from the others, especially the good doctor. Too many people had asked him how he was feeling, and she'd even gone so far as to ask how the pain pills were working. He wouldn't say so, but he was thankful those were once again doing their job. The pain no longer kept him awake at night. Dreams were another matter.

He'd nearly reached the stairs that would take him up to the solitude that would save his sanity, when he heard someone approaching him from behind. Certain it was one of his family coming to see why he'd left, he turned to look, ready to give any answer it took so he could escape. To his surprise, it was his son, Shawn.

"They sure do know how to talk, don't they?" Shawn asked, a smile on his face.

Tucker nodded. "That they do. Enough to wear a person out." He'd learned that if he spent some time with his family, he could use being tired as an excuse.

Shawn stopped a few feet from him, his smile slowly disappearing. "Then I won't keep you long."

"Don't worry about it," Tucker said quickly, wishing he hadn't mentioned being worn-out. That wasn't how he wanted his son to see him. "I'm not that tired."

A brief smile appeared for a moment, before Shawn nodded. "I only wanted to ask you something."

Tucker leaned against the wall to show he wasn't going anywhere. "Sure. Go ahead."

"I have a baseball game on Monday, and I thought maybe you might like to come to it."

Tucker saw the hope in the boy's eyes and couldn't deny this small request. "No reason I can't," he answered with a shrug, although he knew that wasn't completely the truth. He didn't feel comfortable in public, but for Shawn, he'd do anything. "Just remind me. Sometimes I lose track of time."

Shawn's smile lit his entire face. "Great! Yeah, I'll remind you. You don't have to worry about that."

"You're not bronc riding anymore?" Tucker asked.

Shawn shrugged and looked away. "A little. Not as much as I used to."

"Whatever you want to do."

After nineteen years, Tucker had a lot of time to make up. There'd been no communication with his family since he was fifteen and left in search of what he thought would be a better life. Rodeo had been his goal, and he'd wandered the circuit for a couple of years, until he'd discovered it wasn't what he wanted. Or needed. But he hadn't wanted to go back home, either. He wished with all his heart he'd known he had son. It was Shawn who kept him at the Rocking O Ranch now.

"Well," Shawn said, taking a hesitant step back, "that's all I wanted to tell you. I guess I'd better get back."

Shoving away from the wall, Tucker wanted to reach out to him, to let the boy know he loved him. But love wasn't something he knew how to convey. "I'll see you later," he promised.

"Yeah."

Tucker watched him walk away before moving on to conquer the stairs. He always tried to make sure no one saw him going up or down. His worthless left leg made walking difficult enough, but stairs were his undoing. He had no doubt that if Jules knew, other arrangements would be made, but he liked the view from the upstairs bedroom, where he could see the barn and ranch. It gave him a feeling of peace. He wasn't sure why.

By the time he reached the top of the stairs, sweat had broken out on his forehead, and he wiped it away with his forearm. Leaning against the wall once again, he rested. At least his leg wasn't hurting. He knew he had Paige Miles to thank for that, but telling her so wasn't something he was comfortable doing. She was an attractive woman—much too attractive, as far as he was concerned. If he had a better track record when it came to women...

He'd been a charmer when he was young. Shawn was proof of just how charming. From what Tanner had told him, Shawn's young mother had dropped Shawn off with Tanner to raise when Shawn was six months old. Tucker hardly remembered Hollyanne and never knew he'd gotten her pregnant. He'd been sixteen and on an adventure. At the time, adventure meant a roll in the hay when he could get it, with several cans of beer, when available. He was ashamed to think about it. At least he'd matured, even though nothing ever got serious with any of the other women he'd met and dated.

Tucker made his way around the circular hallway to his room. If it wasn't for the stairs, he'd be able to get around without too much trouble, but he wasn't going to say anything to Tanner about that. His brother tended to keep a distance between them, which was fine with

Tucker. Tanner had tried to take the place of their father when they were young and Tucker had taken exception to it. Hated it, was more like it. It had been one of the main reasons he'd left. Now Tanner said little, as if the two of them were strangers.

Lying on the bed, Tucker thought of his childhood, of how his mother had come and gone, then never returned. His father had left the ranch to look for her, certain she was riding the rodeo circuit. But a bull had put an end to Brody O'Brien's search and his life, and had left two young sons alone. If it hadn't been for Brody's twin sister, Bridey, coming to live with them, Tucker knew his life and his brother's would have been very different. They all owed her a lot of thanks.

He hadn't realized he'd fallen asleep, when a knock on the door awakened him. "Everybody's gone, Tucker," he heard Jules say. "Would you like some dessert?"

"Come on in," Tucker said, shifting to sit on the edge of the bed. He looked up when the door opened and saw her walk into the room with a plate of cake in one hand and a glass of tea in the other.

"I can bring you some coffee, if you'd rather," she said, handing him the glass and plate.

"This is fine," he said, and then added, "thanks."

She stood watching him as he placed the food and drink on the small table next to the bed. "We decided to raid the kitchen for supper tonight," she told him. "Can I bring you something later?"

"No, that's okay. I'll get something when I'm hungry," he answered, even though he knew another trip up and down the stairs wouldn't be easy.

"You're sure? It's no trouble for—"

"I'm sure," he said, cutting her off. He hadn't planned

to be a burden to his family, but he couldn't leave, not until after Shawn graduated. With that less than two months away, he didn't have much time to get to know his son and be the kind of dad he'd always hoped to be someday, but he had to try. He couldn't just walk away.

Jules nodded and turned for the door. "Let me know if you need anything."

Tucker waited until she was gone before he picked up the plate and enjoyed the cake. It was a habit he'd formed while being held prisoner and had not yet managed to break, even after nearly a year since he'd been rescued. He'd never imagined that adjusting to life outside a primitive prison cell would be so difficult. But then his focus had been on surviving, not a life of freedom.

Setting the empty plate on the table, he leaned back. Conversations from dinner floated through his mind. Most of them he didn't pay much attention to. And he'd really tried not to be aware of the woman sitting next to him. Unfortunately that hadn't been as easy as he'd hoped.

PAIGE GLANCED AT her watch as she stood inside the clinic doorway. It was after three, and she needed to be at the baseball field. The game would start in less than an hour, and as team physician—a position she'd been surprised to be asked to take over—it was her job to make sure the players on all of the Desperation Desperados teams were in good shape and warmed up before games to avoid injuries. With her car at the service station for a much-needed oil change, she'd asked her brother, Garrett, to pick her up and take her to the game.

He was late, something that rarely happened unless he was tied up in court. If that had happened, there was no telling when he'd be free.

With a sigh of frustration, she opened the door and stepped outside. After making sure the door was locked behind her, she began to walk in the direction of the high school. It wasn't far, and the weather was pleasant, but she hated being late and never accepted appointments in the late afternoon on game days to make certain she would be on time. She'd discovered she enjoyed the extra work with the teams, because it gave her the opportunity to meet the younger generation in Desperation outside of the clinic. Without their parents, they were more honest about themselves and if they were hurting or not.

She hadn't reached the end of the first block when she heard a car honk behind her, and she turned around to see Garrett behind the wheel of his sports car.

"Trouble?" she asked when she opened the car door and scooted inside.

"Sorry," he replied, putting the car into motion. "Something came up."

Sensing her usual charming brother had his mind on other things, she remained quiet during the short ride to the baseball field at the high school. She had enough to think about. One of the boys had been injured at the previous game on Friday and another at practice the day before. Nothing serious, but when it came to the boys and sports, she didn't let anything go.

Garrett pulled into the parking lot and stopped the car near the gate to the field. "Do you want me to come back to get you, or should I stick around?"

"Why don't you stick around?" she suggested, thinking he might enjoy watching the practice. He'd played in high school and some in college, too, and had enjoyed it. Nodding, he shut off the engine, and she reached for the door handle, but something didn't feel right to her. "Garrett?" she asked. "Is everything okay?"

He turned to look at her with his usual good-natured smile. "Yes, mother hen. I'm fine. But you'd better hustle."

Pausing for a moment to study him, she decided she was imagining things. He'd probably been thinking of something that had happened at work. He often said that being the city attorney wasn't all that hard, but there were times he questioned if he'd been sane when he took the job.

"All right," she said, opening her door. "I'll join you after the game starts."

Outside the field near the dugout, she could see the boys gathered around Jim Perkins, the football coach. A strict but fair man, he wouldn't be happy that she hadn't been on time, so she hurried in their direction.

The group broke up as she reached it, and she stopped the team's starting pitcher, before he began his warm-up pitches. "How's your wrist, Ryan?"

Ryan Wells held up his hand and flexed his wrist. "It's good. The ice and bandage over the weekend did the trick."

She nodded and searched the others trotting onto to the field. "Tommy," she shouted when she spied the second boy she'd seen at the clinic, the day before. "Let me look at that eye before you get started."

A big boy, he stopped at the sound of his name and ducked his head as he lumbered toward her. "It's okay, Dr. Paige," he told her.

When he came to a halt in front of her, she reached up and gently touched the swollen area around the cut she'd butterflied the day before. "Tommy James, I told you to keep it iced all night."

He looked at her with eyes widened in innocence in his round, chubby face. "I did!"

"Okay," she answered, nodding, "but you'll need to do it again, as soon as you get home." Putting on her tough face, she frowned. "If you don't, that eye's going to close, and you won't see the ball coming at you, much less the pitcher throwing it."

His head bobbed up and down. "I will, I will. I promise, Dr. Paige."

"Go on, then." As he returned to join the other team members, she smiled and shook her head. Tommy might be a big guy—a real big guy—but he was a teddy bear.

When the team began warming up, she took her time looking over each of them, watching for signs of pain or hesitancy in their movements. As far as she could tell, all were well, but she'd check with them again before the game started.

"Keep an eye on them," Coach Perkins told the new assistant coach, and then walked toward Paige. "You were late."

"Blame Garrett," she said with a shrug of her shoulders. He might intimidate others, but not her. "My car's in the shop, and he was tied up at work."

Instead of answering, the coach looked over her shoulder, squinting his eyes. "Did you ever ask him if he'd be interested in helping out?"

"His schedule won't allow it." She moved to take a

seat on the bench. "He'd want to give it his all, and that isn't possible."

"He was a good player at U of C. One of the best second basemen the division ever had."

"You don't have to tell me." Paige had seen many of her brother's games and had been proud of his athletic ability. But he gave up playing when he decided to go into law instead of medicine, much to their doctor-father's disappointment, on both counts. "If you talked to him, maybe you could get him to come by when he has the time. I think he'd like that."

"Yeah?" the coach asked.

"Yeah."

"Call him over. I'll do that now."

Standing, Paige smiled and turned to the bleachers behind them. She'd never mentioned helping out at practices to Garrett, because she'd known his answer. His schedule was erratic, at times, so there was no reason to mention that the coach would love to have him around. Garrett hated to tell people no. But she also knew how much he'd enjoy helping, so she'd do what she could for him and for the team.

The home team bleachers were beginning to fill with parents and others, in addition to students, who'd come to watch the game and support the team. She searched for her brother and found him seated halfway up the stands, talking to Ryan's dad.

"Hey, Garrett," she called to him, shading her eyes against the late afternoon sun. "Can you come down here?"

Garrett turned to Steve Wells and laughed, then stood to make his way down the bleachers. "What do you need?" he asked Paige.

But before she could answer, someone sitting at the end of the lowest bleacher caught her eye. Tucker had come to watch Shawn.

"Do you need something?" Garrett asked again when he stepped down to the ground.

"Coach wants to talk to you," she answered, but her attention was on Tucker, who appeared to be focused on the team.

"Why?"

Paige's answer was a shrug.

Garrett didn't move. "Something wrong?"

Shaking her head, she looked at him. "Just thinking. Let's go see what Jim wants." Looping her arm through his, she decided to ignore Tucker and walked with Garrett to talk to the coach. There was no reason to suggest PT to Tucker today. He'd made it clear he wasn't interested. It wasn't right to let him get away with causing himself more damage, but she'd pick another time to remind him again. At some point, he might just listen to her. This didn't feel like the time. Besides, seeing him there had unnerved her a little. But she didn't miss that his cane was propped next to him, and she breathed a soft, sad sigh.

Chapter Three

Tucker watched Paige walk away from the stands, unable to tear his gaze away from the smooth swivel of her hips. Shifting on the hard bleacher, he wondered what she was doing there. Considering she'd talked to a couple of the injured players, he guessed she might be the team doctor or something. What he didn't know was who the guy was that she'd called down from the bleachers. Boyfriend?

Frowning, he turned his attention to Shawn, who was talking to the coach. He always felt a swell of pride when he saw his son. For now, it kept his mind off the doctor, something he knew he needed to work on.

"Tucker? Tucker O'Brien?"

Turning, Tucker looked up to see the man who'd spoken to him. "Yeah, that's me."

The man smiled. "You don't remember me. Jimmy Tartelli," he said, offering his hand. "My older brother was in your class in school."

Recognition dawned, as Tucker took the outstretched hand and thought back to his early days in Desperation. "Right! Yeah, I remember Ben. You, too."

"I'll have to let Ben know you're back in town. He's asked about you often."

And you had no answer, Tucker thought. Nobody did. Only his grandmother Ayita knew he'd joined the marines when he turned eighteen, and he'd sworn her to secrecy. "How's Ben doing? Still here in Desperation?"

"No, he's career air force, currently stationed in Qatar."

"I've heard it's beautiful there."

"So he's said. Mind if I sit down?" Jimmy asked.

"Sure, go ahead."

Jimmy moved around Tucker and settled next to him on the bleacher. "If the earlier games are any indication, we have a good team this year. Shawn is a great shortstop."

"I'm looking forward to seeing him play," Tucker replied. When his grandmother had told him he had a son, he'd expected Shawn to be riding broncs or bulls, like the rest of the O'Briens had. Tanner had told him that Shawn had chosen broncs and was damn good, and that he'd team-roped with Dusty. But a couple of years ago, he'd become interested in traditional sports. Tucker didn't mind. From experience, he knew a life of rodeo wasn't easy. His brother might be a national champion bronc rider, but even he'd retired as soon as he'd won that gold championship buckle.

"He's a good kid," Jimmy said, looking toward the field.

"Tanner did a good job raising him." Tucker hated to admit it, considering how he'd resented his older brother trying to play dad when they were young. But it was true. Lots of things could have happened to a motherless boy—as they had with him—but Shawn *was* a good kid, and Tucker had Tanner to thank for it. Maybe someday he and his brother could mend the past and be more like real brothers.

"Do you have kids?" he asked Jimmy.

"Two. A boy, ten, and a girl, eight. Jimmy Jr.—everybody calls him J.J.—insisted that we come today. Says he wants to be just like Shawn."

For the first time in a long time, Tucker felt a chuckle rumble in his chest. "I guess he could do worse."

"He sure could," Jimmy agreed, standing. "And I see Shawn headed this way. I'd better get back to my boy. Good seeing you again, Tucker. Glad you're back."

"Thanks. Good to see you, too. And tell Ben hello for me."

"I will," Jimmy said, before he turned to walk away.

But Tucker's attention was now on his son, who was walking toward him. He wished he'd been around to watch Shawn grow up. His aunt Bridey had shown him pictures of Shawn as a baby—Shawn toddling, riding horses, opening birthday and Christmas presents—but they were only pictures, not the real thing. He'd missed so much.

"Hey, Dad," Shawn called to him, as he approached the far end of the bleachers where Tucker sat.

Tucker grasped at something dadlike to say. "You look good out there."

Shawn's embarrassed grin and quick duck of his head was a sure sign that his ego wasn't bigger than he was. He wore a baseball mitt and was tossing a ball into it. "Thanks. Say, Coach wants me to keep warmed up, and all the other guys are either already paired off or doing something else. Would you mind playing a little catch with me?"

Tucker's gut response was to shout *no,* loud and clear. But what kind of dad would do that? He was being offered the chance to do what every other dad did with his son. But could he do it? If he couldn't, it would be just one more failure to add to his long list.

Before he could answer, one of the other boys trotted up to Shawn and handed him another mitt. Shawn turned to Tucker. "All we'll do is play catch. No running."

It wasn't that Tucker couldn't catch or throw a ball, but he'd have to do it without his cane, and his balance wasn't as good as it could be. The thought of something happening that would not just embarrass him, but Shawn, too, had him hesitating. He didn't want that to happen.

"I'm pretty rusty, Shawn," he said, hoping that would take care of it.

There was a flash of disappointment in Shawn's eyes, before he ducked his head again. "Yeah," he said, with quiet resignation, "I guess you would be."

Tucker's heart nearly broke. Shawn knew he was making excuses. He couldn't do this, no matter what. Somehow he'd have to keep himself upright without help. "But, hey, I can try," came out of his mouth.

Shawn's head came up, and a tentative smile lit his face. "Yeah?"

Shrugging, Tucker mentally crossed his fingers. "Sure."

"Great! That's…that's *great,* Dad."

Knowing he didn't want to get too far away from the bleachers, Tucker grabbed his cane and got to his feet, looking around for a good place to stand.

"How about over there?" Shawn pointed a few yards

away from the bleachers and handed him the extra mitt. "We'll be out of everybody's way."

Not only that, Tucker thought, but he'd also be out of the view of most of the people in the stands. He moved to where Shawn had indicated and dropped his cane on the ground beside him. *Insurance*.

Shawn tossed him the ball, and Tucker caught it easily. Maybe it wouldn't be so bad, and he'd do okay.

He watched Shawn amble out ahead of him several yards, then turn back to face him. "We'll start fairly close," Shawn said, grinning, "until you wear off some of that rust."

"Sounds good." Tucker, still not convinced this was such a great idea, but unable to refuse, tried for his own grin, but suspected he failed. Slamming the ball into his mitt to get a feel for it, he would've prayed all would go well, but he believed he'd used up his quota of prayers in Somalia. Grasping the ball in his right hand, he held it up, ready to throw. Could he remember how to throw? It had been a long time. But his grip felt right, and he'd do his best for Shawn. "Ready?" he shouted.

"Ready."

Cocking his arm back, Tucker threw the ball toward his son, and when Shawn shouted, "Good throw," as he caught the ball, Tucker felt more secure. It wasn't so bad, after all.

Shawn returned the throw, and Tucker caught it without a problem. They continued, and a few throws later, Shawn stepped back farther. "Think you can throw it to the left of me?" Shawn asked. "You know, so I have to reach for it."

Without answering, Tucker threw the ball and it

landed right in Shawn's outstretched glove. "Looks like I can," Tucker answered, feeling more positive.

After a few more throws, Shawn stepped back another two or three yards. Tucker effortlessly threw the ball to him, and Shawn returned the throw.

This time, the throw was a little off as it left Shawn's hand, and Tucker heard him shout, "Sorry about that." Tucker didn't want to miss the throw, no matter how off it might be and he stepped hard to his left.

A wrenching pain shot through his knee, and it was all he could do to keep from going to the ground. But he didn't. No way, he thought, as he closed his eyes and tried to fight off the dizzying pain.

"Dad! Dad!" The fear in Shawn's voice was clear.

Tucker managed to open his eyes enough to see Shawn running to him, but he quickly closed them again, as he focused on staying upright. He hadn't had pain like this since before he'd left the hospital.

He didn't know how much time had gone by when he sensed someone beside him and opened his eyes enough to see Shawn picking up the cane. "I'm sorry, Dad. I didn't know…"

"It's okay, son," Tucker managed to say through clenched teeth. He felt Shawn press the cane to his hand and was grateful that he now had something to lean on and take the weight off his knee.

"Maybe I should get—"

"No!" Tucker didn't want anyone around until he could get the pain under control. But he wondered if he ever would. Then just as he began to manage the pain more easily, he heard a voice.

"There's something you can do about that, you know."

He opened his eyes to see Paige walking by with the man he'd seen her talking to earlier, and he had to grit his teeth harder not to reply.

"What did she say?" Shawn asked.

"Nothing." At least as far as Tucker was concerned.

"Do you want me to go after her? She could take a look—"

"No, that's okay."

Shawn didn't seem convinced. "Okay, but if you aren't better tonight, then you have to promise to go see her tomorrow."

It was the last thing Tucker wanted to do. Instead of answering, he shrugged in response as he carefully made his way back to the bleachers. *Where you should have stayed.*

Following, Shawn sat on the bleachers next to him, once Tucker was seated. "What did she mean?"

"What?" Tucker asked.

"She said something about there was something you could do. What did she mean?"

Tucker didn't want to talk about this with his son. It wasn't Shawn's business. He shook his head.

"Dad?"

Choking back a frustrated sigh, Tucker finally answered. "She wants me to get some physical therapy."

Shawn was silent for a moment, as he studied Tucker. "Will it help?"

Help? Tucker hated the word. There were reasons he didn't want to give therapy a try—very important reasons—and he couldn't tell Shawn, because his son wouldn't understand. He'd spent months in hospitals, and another doctor was something he couldn't deal with. And he didn't believe therapy would help. Therapy wasn't what had gotten him on his feet—to stand, then to take steps. It was because he'd learned he had a son, and there wasn't anything that would keep him from going back to Desperation. Not his leg, not even his resentment of his brother.

"Dad? Will it help?" Shawn asked again.

"I doubt it," Tucker answered, but couldn't look at him.

"But you don't know, right? Why would she suggest it, if she didn't think it would be worth it? I mean, she's a doctor. She knows this stuff. Besides, there's always a chance it might help. So do it."

Tucker was saved from answering when someone shouted to Shawn, reminding him they had a game to play. Tucker watched him walk away. In a few weeks, Shawn would be graduating. After that, Tucker knew Shawn had plans to travel with some friends—plans that had been made long before Tucker had shown up. In the fall, Shawn would be off to college, so these weeks were all he had to spend with his son, to get to know him, to try to learn how to be a father. A dad. Time spent traveling to do therapy somewhere would be time they wouldn't have together, and Tucker couldn't afford that.

But Shawn expected him to at least try. He couldn't let Shawn down. He couldn't let what happened today happen again. He *had* to get help. For Shawn.

THE DAY TOOK A nosedive when Paige looked at the appointment book first thing the next morning and saw Tucker's name as the third appointment of the day. She'd been standing on the baseline near the dugout, talking with some of the players, when Tucker reached for the baseball Shawn had thrown him. There was no doubt he'd suffered some serious pain. She saw his face as his knee gave out. The question was whether he'd done any permanent damage to his knee. But she really hadn't expected him to make an appointment to see her—or to do it so soon.

No, it wouldn't be a good morning. She hated starting the day with a belligerent patient, and Tucker certainly fit that bill. He fit other bills, too, but she wouldn't allow herself to think about them.

Doctor first, woman second, she told herself as she opened the examining room door after seeing her first two patients. It was the one thing she needed to keep in mind, whenever Tucker was around.

Stepping into the room, she did her best not to look directly at him. His brown eyes were always piercing and made her feel like she was undressed. Foolish, she knew, but she hadn't been able to rid herself of the feeling since the barbecue at the O'Briens'. This time she'd do better.

"You had some trouble at the baseball game yesterday," she stated. There was no reason to ask. She'd seen it.

The irresistible urge to tug at her skirt when she dared to look at him and noticed he was looking at her legs was almost more than she could control. But she did.

"I shouldn't have agreed when Shawn asked if I'd help him warm up." His gaze moved upward, until it collided with hers.

Determined to beat down the rush of warmth she

felt, she refused to look away. "And as I told you as I was leaving, there's something you can do about it."

For a moment, he held her gaze, and then he glanced away. "I admit it was my fault. Isn't that enough?"

Paige considered it. "Enough for me? Or enough for you?"

His gaze nailed her again. "Seems you think it isn't enough for you."

She shook her head. "No, it has nothing to do with me, except that I want to help you. I want you to do something about it. But there's no need to point a finger. We're both at fault, at any rate."

"How do you figure that?"

Because he looked sincere about the question, she decided to answer it truthfully. "Maybe I should have *insisted* that you see a physical therapist. Maybe I should have called and made the appointment for you myself."

"But you didn't."

She ignored his reply. "Maybe you should have given it more thought and at least asked for a referral."

He shook his head, as if he had no responsibility in any of it. "I don't like doctors."

Paige couldn't help but smile. "You've made that pretty clear."

"You might feel the same if you'd spent as many months in hospitals as I have, being poked, prodded, cut and stitched."

She nodded slightly. "You may be right." She waited for a response from him, but when he said nothing, she continued. "But in the case of physical therapy, you won't be working with a doctor. You won't be in the hospital, either. You'll make visits, probably every week for several weeks, maybe twice a week, if needed. It won't be the same."

His jaw moved, tightening, before he answered. "That's the other thing." He looked down, then back at her. "I can't do the long drive to Oklahoma City. Now, if there's a therapist nearby—"

"I can check into that."

"But can you make up the time I'd have to spend away from Shawn?"

She was surprised. "Would it be *that* much time? Especially if I can find someone close to Desperation?"

His eyes narrowed in thought. "Maybe not. But if there isn't, then, yes, it is too much time."

"An hour or two a week?"

"Plus driving time. And the driving itself."

Paige understood. They'd been over this on his first visit. Standing, she first made sure her skirt wasn't hiked, and then she picked up his file. "If you have a few minutes to wait, I'll go check with the ladies in the office and see if they can find a physical therapist in the area."

He nodded, but he didn't look convinced or happy at the prospect.

She was out of the room quickly, with her fingers crossed. If she could find someone—anyone—within fifteen miles or so of Desperation, she just might be able to talk Tucker into doing the physical therapy. He needed to feel normal again, to be a whole, undamaged person. Once he was physically better, then he could work on the psychological problems he had. And she had no doubt there were many of those.

"How's it going?" Cara Milton, the clinic's receptionist asked, when Paige stepped into the office.

Paige looked around. "Are Fran and Susan busy?"

"I'm here," Fran said, from behind her. "Susan's getting vitals. Shall I buzz her?"

"Please," Paige answered.

"You might want this." Cara handed Paige an extremely thick packet and glanced at Fran, who was on the phone with Susan.

Paige took the package and looked at the address. It was from Dr. Fuller at the VA in Oklahoma City and obviously Tucker's records. "Thanks. This could help."

"Is he okay?" Cara asked. "I heard he may have been hurt at the game yesterday."

Paige smiled. News spread fast in Desperation, but she wasn't saying anything. She was his doctor. "I'll need an X-ray of his left knee."

Susan Fulcom slipped into the office. "Do you need something?"

Paige addressed all three of them. "Do any of you know if there's a physical therapist in the area? Fifteen miles or less away, if possible?"

"Martha Bentley practiced in Kingfisher for several years," Susan offered, "but she moved away a few years ago. To the West Coast, I think, lucky woman."

Paige still held hope that one of them would know someone. "Anyone else?" All three women shook their heads. "All right. I was hoping, that's all."

Back in the examining room, she tossed the package Cara had given her onto the counter.

"What's that?" Tucker asked.

Paige turned to him. "Your medical records."

"How did you get them?"

"You signed a release when you were here last week. Don't you remember?"

"No."

She knew he'd been in pain, so it didn't surprise her that he had no recollection of signing anything. "Then maybe I should ask if it's all right if I look through them."

He didn't look directly at her when he shrugged. "What did you find out about a therapist?"

Paige hated giving bad news more than anything. And she knew he wouldn't accept this well. "There isn't one in the area. You'll need to go to Oklahoma City."

Disappointment flashed in his eyes—deep disappointment. He reached for his cane. "Then that's that."

As he moved off of the examining table, she saw him wince. "Tucker…" He turned to look at her, and she knew she couldn't say what she should. "Are the pain pills helping?"

"Some. At least they were."

She couldn't let him leave, not until they knew the score about his injury. "We should x-ray your knee," she said, before he could take another step. His frown deepened, and she quickly added, "To see if there's any damage."

It was as if she'd told him he was terminal. "Damage? To what they fixed?"

Nodding, she wished she could skip this. If there was damage done— She didn't want to think about it. Another surgery wouldn't be something he'd embrace with joy. "Do you have the time? It won't take long. Your latest X-rays are probably in here." She tapped on the package beside her on the counter. "I can compare the two sets and determine if there's any new damage."

He nodded. "I'd rather know than not know."

Relief flooded through her. "Good. Stay right here, and we'll get on it immediately. I promise not to keep you much longer."

Twenty minutes later, as she compared the new X-rays with the last ones taken at the VA, she felt weak with relief. At least she had some good news for Tucker.

"No damage," she told him, when she walked into the examining room.

His relief was visible. "So now what?"

"Were you given a knee brace?" When he nodded, she smiled. "Wear it. And ice that knee for the rest of the day. I'll give you a prescription for an anti-inflammatory. Get it filled and start taking it."

He didn't move as she'd expected he would. "What about the therapy?" he asked.

"It all comes down to going to Oklahoma City. I'm sure we can find you a good therapist there. It doesn't have to be at the VA."

His deep brown eyes revealed nothing. "Why can't you do it?"

Paige was speechless. He thought *she'd* do it? Why in the world would she do that? He'd freely admitted that he didn't like doctors, so why choose her? Why put her through all of this, and then ask something like that of her? And that was just the beginning. There was also that fact that—

"Well?"

"I— No, I can't." She turned to the cabinet, as if there was something there of great importance, hoping to ignore the thoughts racing through her mind.

"Why not?" he asked from behind her.

Taking a deep breath, she turned to face him again. "Because I'm a general practitioner. I'm neither an orthopedist nor a physical therapist."

"It makes a difference?"

She swallowed. "In this case, yes." But for reasons she wasn't willing to share. She was attracted to him, although she'd never admit it to anyone. She shouldn't even be treating him, if she was completely honest with herself. Dealing with his therapy would be more than she wanted to tackle, not only because of his attitude and that attraction she felt, but she also didn't believe he'd stick with it.

He grabbed his cane and stood down from the examining table. "Think about it."

She stared as he opened the door and walked out. When he was gone, she breathed out a long, loud sigh. She'd be crazy to even consider doing his therapy.

"WHERE DOES Paige Miles live?"

Jules turned from the refrigerator and looked at Tucker. "Paige? Why?"

Tucker was fairly certain Jules didn't know about the therapy thing—at least he hoped not—and he wasn't about to tell her. "I need to talk to her."

Jules's eyebrows shot up.

"I can show you," Shawn announced, walking into the kitchen.

Tucker didn't miss the smile on Jules's face before he turned to his son. "Can you just tell me? It's not like I don't know the streets in Desperation."

Shawn shot him a quirky smile. "I guess you do. Turn

right at the drugstore, then go three blocks. It's the brick house on the left with white trim. She lives—"

"Thanks," Tucker answered, and grabbed the keys to the pickup. "I'll be back later."

He'd spent the rest of the day before, after he'd seen Paige, with an ice pack on his knee. He'd even watched a little television with the family, and then turned in early. When he woke up, he felt almost as good as he had before he'd twisted his knee playing catch with Shawn. Almost. The prescription and ice seemed to be doing the trick. Maybe even the knee brace he'd dug out of an unpacked duffel bag was helping. He wasn't sure. He didn't care, he was just glad.

Most of the morning he'd spent doing research on Tanner's computer. He hoped his brother, who was fixing fences with Dusty and Rowdy, didn't mind. He found the information he needed.

The spring evening was beginning to settle in as he drove into town. He'd forgotten how pretty Desperation could be. After turning at the corner where Shawn had directed, he searched for the brick house with white trim and hoped he'd timed his visit right. Parking the truck across from the house, he noticed there wasn't a car in the drive. There also didn't appear to be any lights on inside, so he'd wait and hope it wasn't too long before Paige came home.

He hadn't been waiting for more than five minutes when a sports car turned into the drive. The guy he'd seen with Paige at the baseball game climbed out on the driver's side, doubling Tucker's curiosity. Boyfriend or…husband? No, he didn't think she was married. He'd never seen a ring on her finger or even an indentation of one having been there.

He wasn't sure what to think as he ignored his disappointment, and then another car, fairly new and a bit classy, slowed and pulled into the drive to park next to the sports car. Climbing out of the pickup, he closed the door and started across the street. The guy and Paige, who was getting out of the second car, both turned to look at him.

"Tucker?" Paige asked when he walked up the drive. "What are you doing here?"

He slid a look at the guy, standing nearby. "I wanted to talk to you."

Turning to the guy, she waved him on. "It's okay. Go on inside."

With a shrug, the guy walked to the house and went inside, but not without looking back, as if he was suspicious of something.

"Would you like to come in?" she asked Tucker.

He wasn't eager to have the conversation in the middle of Paige's front lawn, so he nodded. "If it's... okay."

Paige started for the house and turned back to look at him. "Why wouldn't it be okay?"

Should he say it? Yeah, he should. "Your boyfriend won't mind?"

"My—" She seemed to choke on a laugh. "That's my brother. Haven't you met him?"

Tucker felt foolish, but he also felt a weight lift, although he didn't know why he should. He wasn't interested in her. Except for those chocolate-brown eyes of hers. And those legs. And that—

He shook his head and followed her. "You don't look like brother and sister, so I thought..."

"Garrett takes after Mom, and I take after Dad." She

opened the door and stepped inside, motioning for him to follow. "I guess you haven't had any run-ins with the law."

"Not since I was fourteen," he answered, as he followed her. "But I thought Morgan Rule was the sheriff."

"He is. Garrett is the city attorney."

Inside, he saw her brother in the living room, removing his suit jacket, and immediately decided to reserve judgment, until he knew him better.

"So you're both transplants," he said, not knowing what else to say.

"Afraid so," her brother said, walking toward him with an outstretched hand. "Garrett Miles. It's good to meet you, Tucker."

Tucker returned the handshake and decided her brother was okay. "Hope you like it here," he told Garrett. "Some folks don't care much for small-town living."

"It beats city life," Garrett said with a friendly smile.

"Garrett is the one who coerced me into moving here from Chicago," Paige explained.

"It took a while," Garrett said, turning to Paige, who answered with a nervous smile, "but big brother always wins out." He smiled and he winked at her before facing Tucker again. "You'll have to excuse me. It took me forever to get her to move here. She can be very stubborn at times, but I don't think she'd leave for anything." After glancing at a glaring Paige, he laughed. "I'd tell you more interesting tidbits about my sister, but I have work to do, so I'll leave you two alone."

When he was gone, Paige turned to Tucker. "You'll have to excuse Garrett. He was kind enough to share his house with me when I came to Desperation, but sometimes he forgets he's not in court. Please, sit down and tell me why you're here."

Tucker hoped it would be that easy. He doubted it would be, but he sat on the sofa, while she perched on the arm of a chair. "I've been doing some research," he began. "The internet is amazing."

"Yes, it is."

He knew she was waiting for an explanation, so he pushed on. "There's no reason why you can't do my physical therapy."

Her eyes widened, and then she shifted on the arm of the chair. "I already told you—"

"Yeah, you did, but I'm a little more informed now. You've had some training, right?"

Her nod was slow. "I did an orthopedic rotation and had some basic physical therapy training, but—"

"Then there's no reason why you can't."

She popped off the chair like someone had shot her. After pacing to the other side of the room, she turned to face him. "You have to understand that because you haven't participated in the therapy you should have, your muscles have probably begun to atrophy. To some degree, anyway."

"That's not uncommon after ACL surgery."

This time her eyebrows shot up. He had her.

"I'll lay it on the line," he said, leaning back. "I don't trust doctors. For some reason, I trust you. You have enough training, and if anything is wrong, as a doctor, you'd know it and treat it. So it comes down to one thing."

"And that is?"

He answered slowly and clearly, so she wouldn't

misunderstand. "I'll do the physical therapy, if you'll be the therapist."

He'd heard about the deer-in-the-headlights reaction, but he'd never seen it done—and done so well.

Chapter Four

Paige had every intention of saying no, of refusing his request to oversee his physical therapy, but instead of doing that, she pressed her lips together and said nothing. An internal dialogue whispered through her mind at light speed.

Of course she couldn't do what he asked.

But if she didn't help, he wouldn't get the therapy he needed.

Her practice kept her busy. She didn't have time to oversee his therapy.

A once-a-week check on his progress wouldn't take more than ten or fifteen minutes. Surely she could spare that much for a patient.

She'd already admitted to herself that she was attracted to him. Okay, more than simply attracted. Maybe. Spending even that small amount of time with him once a week or so was a bad idea. Now was the time to put a halt to it.

He needed medical help. She was a doctor. How could she refuse his request and live with herself?

"Well?" he asked, ending the back-and-forth in her mind.

She forced herself to look at him, still not ready to make a decision. "I don't know."

Without a sound, he lowered his head. His broad shoulders straightened before he raised it again. "Then I guess I'll do it on my own."

"No!" She couldn't allow him to do that. He could cause more damage to his knee, and it would be her fault if he did. "I'll—" She took a deep breath and let it out on a long sigh. "You leave me no choice. I'll do it." As soon as she said it, the strain on his face and the stiffness in his shoulders eased. Her strain, however, increased. "But with reservations and some rules," she added, not wanting him to feel he'd won the war. He'd only won this one battle. She suspected it wouldn't be the last.

He nodded. "All right."

Now that she'd made the decision, she was determined that it would work out. She would be in charge from here on out. "You'll have to agree to follow my instructions to the letter."

He shrugged. "I can do that. I've been doing that in one way or another most of my life. This won't be any different."

She highly doubted they would get through this ordeal without him questioning her at every opportunity or just being downright stubborn and argumentative. He'd certainly proved he was a pro at it. "No excuses, no arguments. I'm in charge."

"You're the doctor."

She nodded, hoping she appeared more positive and sure of herself than she was feeling. In fact, she felt more like a fool than a doctor, but it was too late to change that now.

"When do we start?" he asked.

In for a penny, in for a pound. "Call the clinic first thing in the morning and make an appointment for Friday. We'll start then."

Grabbing his cane, he pushed to his feet, struggling for a brief moment, until he was standing straight and steady. "How long do you think this will take?"

As little time as possible, she wanted to answer. "A month. Two months," she said, "or more, depending on how dedicated you are." She suspected it wouldn't be long before he quit. "There'll be some pain, at least in the beginning."

"I can deal with it."

She didn't doubt he could, but she also knew that PT after ACL surgery wasn't a picnic. She didn't know if he was up for that. "We'll just have to see how it goes," she said, not realizing she'd spoken.

He'd started to turn toward the front door, but he hesitated. "Are you doubting me or yourself?" he asked.

She didn't know. What she did know was that she'd agreed to do something she wasn't certain was the right thing to do. "Maybe both," she answered, as honestly as she could, then wished she hadn't said it.

His gaze burned into her, his expression unreadable. "It's a good thing *I* have faith in one of us."

"Yes," she answered as he walked to the door. But which one? And did she really want to know?

He said nothing as he reached the door and opened it. A quick glance back at her, and then he was gone.

Relieved and filled with dread at the same time, she lowered herself slowly to the chair.

"All done?"

She looked up to see Garrett standing just inside the

living room, having come from his office down the hall. How could she have been so crazy to agree to Tucker's request? "Only beginning, I'm afraid," she answered.

Her brother walked farther into the room. "How so?"

"I've agreed to act as his physical therapist."

"Is that a bad thing?"

She wondered. As long as she kept it strictly on a professional level, maybe it would all work out for the best. She'd feel better about herself, and Tucker would walk without a cane.

"Of course it isn't," she answered Garrett. She only hoped the determination she'd seen in Tucker's eyes would carry them through this, however long it might take. She wasn't ready to bank on it, though. In fact, she expected him to be a no-show on Friday.

TUCKER POURED HIMSELF a second cup of coffee, then leaned back against the kitchen counter and silently watched his family begin the day. When he'd first arrived at the ranch, he'd been amazed to discover that each family member had his or her own role in the morning madness. He didn't. After a month of living with them, he still didn't feel as if he was a part of the family. But why should he? When he'd left all those years ago, never looking back, there'd been no plans to return.

Plans changed. He should've known they would.

"I'll be at the Bent Tree most of the day," Jules announced as she buttered a slice of toast. "Linda and I want to have everything in order when Nikki and Mac get back from their honeymoon."

Tanner laughed, taking his seat next to her at the

table. "Some honeymoon, traipsing all over the country, visiting equine assisted therapy programs."

"That's our Nikki," Jules answered with a smile.

Bridey entered, carrying a full plate of French toast. "Looks like rain out there," she said, placing the plate in the center of the table.

Shawn was right behind her. "It better not. I hate it when a game gets canceled." As Bridey took a seat, Shawn turned to Tucker. "Can you come?"

"To the game?" Tucker asked. When Shawn nodded, Tucker answered. "I'm not sure. I have—" He didn't plan on telling the family, especially his son, that he was hoping his leg and knee would be better with physical therapy. He'd disappointed them enough. "I may have some things to do, so it depends."

Shawn reached for a piece of French toast. "What things?" Before Tucker could think of an answer, a car horn honked. "There's Ryan," Shawn said. "Is there—?"

"Right here," Bridey said, handing him a paper plate and plastic fork.

"Thanks." Shawn plopped his toast on the plate, squirted syrup on it, kissed her cheek and grabbed his books from the countertop. Rushing out of the room with a wave, he called over his shoulder, "See you later."

For a moment the room was quiet. "He's like a small tornado in the morning," Bridey said.

Tanner chuckled quietly. "More like a big one, these days."

"I'm going to miss that," Jules admitted. "But I'm sure Wyoming will do his best to make up for it."

"He will," Tanner replied with a proud father's smile. "And in sixteen years we'll be doing this again."

Tucker's heart ached for the time he'd missed with his son. If he could do it all over again... But he couldn't, and it didn't do any good to look back. All he could do was spend as much time as he could with Shawn now.

Tanner broke the ensuing silence. "Tucker, we could use another eye today with the bulls, if you have time."

Tucker thought about it and nodded. "Be happy to. This morning, anyway."

"Good. We'll get started in about twenty minutes."

Jules looked at Tucker with a strange expression on her face. He knew that look. She had questions. Or maybe concerns. One or the other. Sometimes she voiced them. Sometimes she didn't. This time she wasn't able to, thanks to Rowdy stepping into the room.

"The boys should be arriving any time," he told Tanner.

Tanner pushed away from the table and stood. "You grab some breakfast, and I'll go on out."

"I won't be long," Rowdy said, taking a seat and scooting up to the table.

Tanner turned to Tucker. "Whenever you're ready."

Tucker nodded. "I need to grab a different shirt first."

Nodding, Tanner moved to kiss Jules on the cheek, then left.

After taking a last sip of coffee, Tucker rinsed his cup in the sink and started for his room. But as he stepped into the hallway, he felt someone touch his arm and turned to find Jules.

"I don't mean to pry," she began, "but I worry about you."

Tucker instantly stiffened, but knowing Jules had a good heart, he waited. "There's no need to."

She smiled, but obviously wasn't convinced. "And I worry about Shawn. I heard about what happened at the game the other day."

Tucker frowned. Of course everyone knew. What did he expect in a small town? "I'm fine."

"If you say so, but that's not what concerns me the most. I don't want to see Shawn get hurt. You weren't trying to put him off a few minutes ago because of what happened, were you?"

"No. I have to be somewhere this afternoon."

She waited, as if he was going to explain, and when he didn't, she gave a brief nod. "All right."

When she turned to walk away, he stopped her. "I'm not going to do anything to hurt him, you know. I've already done enough of that."

"I know you'd never mean to," she answered without looking at him.

He watched as she left him standing there, and then he turned for the stairs, shaking his head. He knew she meant well, especially where Shawn was concerned. But this was his chance—his only chance—to get to know the boy he'd fathered. He didn't intend to screw it up.

While changing into a work shirt in his room, after a climb up the stairs made a little easier with the knee brace, and pain pills to ease what wasn't easier, the windows shook with a loud clap of thunder. Seconds later, rain could be heard on the roof. Tucker knew Shawn would be disappointed not to be able to play ball later that day, but Tucker was secretly glad he might have a better chance to see Shawn play if the game was postponed.

Even though he'd called the clinic early the day before to make an appointment, he'd thought he wouldn't be able to get in when he learned that the clinic closed early on high school game days. He was finally squeezed in after the last regular appointment of the day and suspected Paige had made a small concession. He was sure she expected him to be a no-show, but he was going to prove her wrong. When he made the decision to do therapy, he'd vowed to stick with it. He wasn't at all convinced it would do any good, but the doctor was certain there'd be improvement. No matter what he thought, he didn't want to be a fool and pass up what might be the chance to be even a little better.

THE SHADES WERE DRAWN at the doctor's office downtown when Tucker walked up to the door. As he reached to pull the handle, he heard a hard metallic click and the door opened.

"Come on in," the nurse said when she'd opened the door. "Some people seem to think that if a game is a rain-out, the doctor will be in. We do our best to discourage that. If we didn't, Dr. Paige would never get away."

Tucker nodded and stepped inside. With the shades drawn and the lights out, the waiting room was bathed in semidarkness. He followed the nurse as they made their way down a dark hallway toward the back of the clinic, past the examining rooms.

At the end of the hallway, she tapped on a closed door and opened it. "Tucker is here, Doctor."

Paige, standing at a desk on the far side of the room, looked up. "Thank you, Susan," she said with a smile.

Susan glanced at Tucker. "Do you need me to stay?" she asked the doctor.

"No exam today," she answered, shaking her head. "I'll just be showing him how to use the CPM machine and explaining what needs to be done."

"All right, then," Susan answered with a nod. "I'll see you in the morning."

"Watch for deep water on the way home," Paige called to her as she left the room. After writing something in the file that lay open on the desk, she turned to Tucker and pointed to a bench across the room. "Have a seat over there."

Tucker did as she instructed and waited. Several minutes later, Paige left the desk and walked toward him. "Did you say something about a CPM machine?" he asked.

Paige stopped at the examining table near him and leaned against it. "Yes, we'll be using that for your therapy. Not only will that help with your knee, I'm hoping that in the long run, it'll strengthen your lower leg, too. I'm sure that leg is a bit shorter than the other, but that can be improved with the right exercises."

Nodding, Tucker thought about it, but didn't comment.

"You're in good shape," she continued, "in spite of what you've been through and your reluctance to follow doctors' orders. We're basically starting from scratch with some challenges that aren't the norm. We'll know more in a couple of weeks, when I can gauge how quickly your leg and knee are responding to the therapy."

Was there a chance he might be a little better off than he was or that in a few months he'd be walking without a limp and without pain? He was convinced that if his injuries had been treated sooner, everything might be different, but they hadn't been.

"Will I be coming here every day to use the machine?" he asked, imagining how that would be. Probably not as bad as he'd first thought. The doctor was easy on the eyes, if nothing else.

"No, you'll be doing it on your own."

He stared at her. "And just how will I do that?"

"That's what the CPM machine is for. It's the stiffness and swelling, although mostly the stiffness, that causes you the pain. The machine will slowly and constantly work out that stiffness, giving you more flexibility, and do it with ease. And if you follow my instructions, it should be relatively painless."

"That's a plus," he said, before he realized he'd spoken. But he was a little disappointed that he wouldn't be working with her one-on-one. "Are you sure a more personal approach isn't needed?"

"Studies have shown that whether by machine or physical therapist, the outcome is the same, as well as the time it will take."

He hadn't been ready to hear this, but he'd accept it. "How will I know if it's working right?"

"Other than it won't take long for you to notice that your knee will bend more easily, you'll need to come in once, maybe twice a week for measurements so I can tell how much improvement and flexibility you've gained."

"I can do that." In fact, he thought, he almost looked forward to it. But he suspected that if he had to look into those soft brown eyes very often, he'd be finding excuses to see her more often. Not a good idea. Not for a loner like him.

"Are you ready to take a look at the machine?" she asked. When he nodded, she moved across the room and motioned for him to join her there. As he did, she uncovered the strange-looking contraption. He stood next to her and she demonstrated how to place his leg into it and explained the length of time and how often he should use it each day.

"It doesn't look all that hard," he said, when she finished.

"It isn't. The machine does all the work." She also showed him some simple exercises to build muscle strength and help increase range of motion.

He decided he hadn't done enough research, because he wasn't sure what was going to be happening. "So I take it home and use it there, not here?"

"Right." She walked to the desk and picked up the folder, then returned, handing it to him. "Everything I've told you and more is in there. You can always call, if you have any questions or problems."

"Then we're done?"

She nodded. "I'll help you take it out to your…"

"I drove the truck," he finished. Reaching for the machine, he looked at her. "Just how heavy is this?"

"Forty pounds or less."

"Not a problem."

She took the folder from him. "Whenever you're ready to leave…"

"Sure."

"I'll get the door for you."

She followed him down the hallway, unlocking and

opening the main door for him when they reached it. "It's still raining," she said and hurried to open the passenger side door of the pickup. "You do need to keep it dry."

When he'd put the machine in the truck and closed the door, he turned to her. "Do I need to make another appointment?" he asked. A part of him hoped he'd be back, but another part knew it was better to stay away from her. He couldn't explain it, but he was drawn to her, though he knew he couldn't be involved in a relationship, even if he wanted to have one, which he didn't. Just one more thing he'd failed at throughout his life.

"No appointment. Checking your flexion isn't a physician thing." She glanced away. "It will have to be kept off the record, so to speak. You aren't a patient, per se."

"Whatever you say," he answered, but he hoped she wouldn't be getting into any trouble. After all, he had pushed her hard to do this. "I'll take all responsibility. Does that help?"

"It does," she said, smiling. "We'll do the first check on Tuesday evening. Meet me here about seven. It won't take long."

"I'll do that," he said, nodding. "And... Well, thanks for all this. I know you didn't have to do it."

"Just don't give up on it," she answered.

He nodded and walked around the front of the truck to the driver's side. As he opened the door, he looked up to see her standing on the sidewalk, watching him. "One more thing," he said.

The rain had turned to a mist, and she wrapped her arms around herself. "What's that?"

"I'd appreciate it if you don't mention this to anyone.

Especially my family," he added. "I don't want them to expect miracles and be disappointed. I've been enough of a disappointment."

He started to climb in the truck, but her voice stopped him. "Tucker?"

"Yeah?" he answered, his good right leg already in the truck.

"You aren't a disappointment. They care for you. A lot."

He wasn't going to debate the issue with her. He knew his brother too well not to know that he'd been a sore spot to Tanner for many years. Just one more reason why he didn't plan to hang around after Shawn graduated.

"THANKS FOR STOPPING BY, Paige," Jules said as they walked back to the O'Briens' house.

"No thanks needed," Paige replied. "I always enjoy visiting the boys at the Bent Tree. I can't believe how much they've all changed since the first of them arrived at the ranch last year."

"I really feel we're helping."

"There's no doubt about that," Paige assured her. "It's easy to see what a happy bunch they are." She was amazed at the good things that were being done at the Bent Tree Boys Ranch. Not long after she and Jules had first met, Jules had told her about her longtime dream of providing a safe place for troubled boys who, as Jules put it, had slipped through the cracks of the system. Thanks to Tanner's generosity, Jules's dream had come true, and they were now helping over a dozen boys at the ranch adjacent to the O'Briens' Rocking O Ranch.

They reached the drive where Paige had left her car,

and Jules stopped her. "Didn't you say Garrett is out of town this weekend?"

"He's at a seminar in Dallas," Paige answered. "I expect him home sometime tomorrow."

"Then why don't you stay for supper? There's no reason for you to go home to an empty house."

Paige laughed. "I'm used to an empty house. Garrett's hours tend to be even later than mine. We hardly ever see each other, which is probably why we get along."

Jules laughed, too. "Then there really isn't a reason for you to go home early. We'll have plenty. Bridey's fixing fried chicken."

"With all the fixings?" Paige asked, her watering mouth betraying her.

"All of them," Jules answered with a wicked smile.

Paige shaded her eyes with her hand and looked toward the house. "It's tempting," she admitted. "Tanner's aunt is such a wonderful cook, and it's been a long time since I've had home-cooked fried chicken." She looked at Jules. "You're sure it's no trouble?"

"None at all. The men are over helping a neighbor put up fence. I don't expect them back for quite a while, and Bridey promised to heat everything for them when they get home."

Knowing Tucker and the others wouldn't be around was what made the difference. Although she and Tucker hadn't had any problems at his appointment the day before, she hadn't felt completely comfortable with him. She guessed he felt the same.

"All right," she said, "but I can't stay late."

"Great! Let's go in and see if we can help Bridey with anything, although I have a feeling she won't allow us in the kitchen until everything is ready."

Paige followed her up the porch steps and then around the covered porch to the back, where they entered through double doors that led into the dining room. From there, Paige was lost. "I grew up in a big house," she said, still following, "but how do you keep from getting lost with all the twists and turns of this one?"

"All of the rooms fan out from the center on both floors," Jules explained. "But I'll admit it took some time to get used to it. The original structure was Tanner and Tucker's childhood home. As time went by, he added to it, a little at a time."

"No one would know by looking at it. It appears almost new."

When they stepped into the kitchen, Bridey was busy cooking, just as Jules had said she would be. "Paige is joining us, Bridey," Jules said. "Is there anything we can do to help?"

Bridey, gathering items from a nearby cabinet, shook her head. "Other than set the table, there's not much left to do. And it won't be long until the food is done."

"There's certainly a lot of that." Paige looked around at various pots and pans, and the extralarge skillet from where the delicious aroma of chicken drifted to make her mouth water.

"The O'Brien men have appetites that don't quit," Bridey answered.

"But I thought—"

"Why don't we set the table?" Jules suggested as she began pulling plates from another cabinet.

Paige agreed and began helping. Just as they were finishing and Bridey was putting food on the table,

Paige heard a sound from outside. "Are you expecting someone?"

Jules shook her head. "Why do you ask?"

"I thought I heard a car. Probably my imagination."

"Oh, I'm sure it was."

But it wasn't imagination when they heard the heavy footsteps and deep voices of men. A few moments later, Tanner walked into the dining room, followed by Rowdy, Shawn and Tucker. Paige wasn't happy, certain Jules had known all along. But it was too late to escape, so she took her seat at the table and tried to mask her annoyance.

Having Shawn sit next to her at the table made the meal easier to endure than it had been the week before, when she'd been seated next to Tucker.

Had it been just over a week since they'd met? He was doing his best to ignore her, and was succeeding. Only twice during the meal did their gazes meet.

When dinner was over—a dinner she was glad she hadn't missed—the men wandered away, one by one, first Tucker, then Shawn and finally Tanner and Rowdy. As she helped Jules clear the table, while Bridey began cleanup in the kitchen, she decided it was time to take a stand with her friend.

"I really enjoy the time I get to spend with your family," she began.

"We enjoy having you," Jules replied.

Paige hated to spoil the mood, but she wanted to get it over with now, instead of later. "The thing is, Jules, there's something that bothers me."

"What's that?" Jules asked.

"It's this matchmaking you're doing."

"Matchmaking? I guess I don't understand."

Paige stared at her, unable to believe Jules was serious. "The pairing off of Tucker and me," she explained, even though she felt uneasy saying it.

"You don't like him?"

"Of course I like him." Pressing her lips together, Paige wished she had put that another way. By the smile on Jules's face, it was clear she was pleased. "Not in that way," Paige hurried to insist.

Jules shrugged as she picked up two more plates. "It's only natural to pair people off. We don't mean anything by it."

"It doesn't matter." Paige sighed, wondering how she could explain. "It's not like this is a big city, where I wouldn't be running into patients at every turn. I do. Daily. And I understood that when I agreed to take over for Doc Priller. In fact, one of the things I thought ran along the lines of who was I going to date when I'm everyone's doctor?"

Jules set the plates on the table and placed her hand on Paige's arm. "There's no reason—"

"Not dating doesn't bother me, Jules. I'm so busy, I don't know where I'd find the time for a relationship. And just so you understand, whether it's because you might have this crazed notion that I can work miracles with Tucker or whether it's simply because we're both available, I'm not interested." Now that she'd begun, she had to finish. "And speaking of Tucker… Well, he has more problems than I want to deal with right now. Probably ever."

"I admit—we all admit—he has some baggage."

"Some?" It was laughable enough that Paige giggled. "He has a whole *boxcar* of baggage."

"Yes, I suppose he does," Jules agreed with a rueful smile.

But Paige wasn't listening. Instead, her face was flushed with the heat of embarrassment. Tucker stood just in the doorway of the room, having obviously heard what she said.

Chapter Five

A boxcar full of baggage, huh? Just who did she think she was? But Tucker couldn't move, in spite of the verbal slap in his face.

"Tucker... I—" Clearly embarrassed, considering the shade of red her face had become, Paige glanced behind her at Jules before trying again. "I didn't mean it like it sounded. I meant—"

"It's all right, Paige," Jules said, putting an arm around her shoulders and patting her arm. "I'm sure Tucker understands that you were joking." She gave Tucker a quick warning glance.

But all he could do was stand there and stare at the doctor. There was no response he could give to that kind of putdown. Of course he wasn't supposed to hear it. She wasn't that cruel. But he had. Maybe it was better to know what she really thought. He'd put a stop to some of those ridiculous thoughts he'd been having about her.

With nothing to say, he turned and walked away. Behind him he heard Jules call his name, but he didn't stop. He'd been insulted by some of the best. Marine drill sergeants were at the top of that list. But he'd never felt as insulted as he had at that moment.

He wasn't in the mood to tangle with the stairs, so

instead of going up to his room—where he should have gone to begin with—he headed for the front door. With each step he took, his anger grew. He didn't try to stop it.

Once outside, he bounded down the front steps, not even thinking of where he might be going, while Paige's words continued to ring in his ears. The earth beneath his boots was spongy from the rain the day before, but it didn't slow him as he crossed the big yard.

Without realizing it, he found himself entering the horse barn and was instantly slammed back into a past he thought he'd forgotten. The smell of hay hit him first as he closed the side door behind him. He heard a soft whinny to his left and farther down the wide aisle. A ray of the last of the day's sunshine fanned out through a small window nearby, and bits of dust danced as he walked through it.

There was a loud bang, and he instinctively spun around and ducked down.

"Haven't seen you in here since you came back."

At the sound of the voice, he realized there was no need to hide. Rowdy wasn't the enemy. "I hadn't planned to be in here," he answered, straightening.

"Any reason why not?"

He could see Rowdy now, another beam of light hitting the ranch foreman as he stepped out of one of the stalls. Tucker couldn't remember a time when Rowdy hadn't been at the ranch. "I try not to live in the past," he finally said.

Rowdy's boot heels clicked as he walked toward Tucker. "The past is what brought us to who and where we are now."

Sighing, Tucker shook his head. How could he tell

this man what his recent past had been like? How could he tell him that his ready advice of long ago was one of the things that had sent him away. Rowdy was known to have a hot temper, and because Tucker had been a boy of action, not thinking, that hot temper had been directed at him more times than not.

"I'm thinking you've been through some things that only forgetting will bring peace."

Tucker couldn't answer and only nodded.

"This is a good place to do it."

Tucker looked at Rowdy. "Not for me."

Rowdy stared back, then shrugged. "I guess you'd know better than me about that, but as far as I know, you're the only one who's ever thought that way." After another shrug, he walked away. But when he'd taken a few steps, he stopped and looked back over his shoulder. "Family horses are down on this end," he explained, pointing toward the big double doors he began walking toward again, "if you get the urge to ride."

Tucker answered without thinking. "It's been too long."

"You never lose it, boy. You know that. But I'm not sure how good you'll do with that thing on your knee. I guess trying is the only way to find out. 'Course your attitude could use some help, too."

Before Tucker could think of a reply, Rowdy was gone, but not without that comment about his attitude, Tucker noted. Same old Rowdy. But Tucker wondered how the old guy knew about the knee brace.

He was pretty certain he hadn't forgotten how to ride, even though he hadn't been on a horse since he was eighteen. Once he'd been accepted into the Marine

Corps, everything had changed for him. That's the way he'd wanted it. A clean break. A new life.

But when he heard the whinny of one of the family horses, he couldn't resist walking down to take a look. They were beauties. Not that he didn't think they wouldn't be. The O'Briens always had the best horses. They took good care of them, too.

His intention was to take a quick look, then be on his way, but when a sorrel gelding, with a white star on his nose, hung his head over the gate just as Tucker walked by, the urge to reach out and touch the animal couldn't be resisted.

"Somebody should put names on the gate," Tucker said, keeping his voice down. "Not that it matters."

But his conversation with the horse ended quickly when he heard the sound of a vehicle being started, and he was jerked back to the present and the incident with his doctor.

If Paige Miles didn't think any better of him than she'd voiced to his sister-in-law, maybe working with her on his therapy wasn't such a good idea. He'd sensed a reticence in her since he'd first asked if she could do the therapy. He just hadn't thought it was important.

Quickly pushing open one of the big doors, he looked to the driveway where he'd seen her car parked when he and the others had returned home for dinner. As he'd thought, it was her car starting that he'd heard. Jules was standing at the driver's door, and he suspected Paige was still apologizing. Now was his chance, before she left, to tell her to forget about the therapy. What difference did it make? It probably wouldn't help anyway.

As he hurried in their direction, as quick as he could with a leg held by knee brace, Jules looked up in his direction. Her frown was evident, but it didn't stop him. It was time to get out of something he should have known was a bad idea.

"Oh, dear," he heard Paige whisper when he reached the car.

He was ready to tell her straight out, even with Jules there, but when he saw the bright red of embarrassment spreading across Paige's cheeks, he couldn't do it. He *did* have a boxcar full of baggage. What a prize he'd turned out to be. A booby prize. It was far from what he'd planned that his life would be, all those years ago, but he was stuck with it, thanks to his own choices. But just because he had some baggage from his past, what gave her the right to think he wasn't good enough for her? That just burned his britches and he'd tell her so.

But before he could speak, he remembered that he was doing the therapy for his son. The boy deserved more than half a man for a father. He'd begun working with the CPM the night before and following her instructions to the letter. If he quit now— No. He was going to see this through.

"Tucker, I'm really—" Paige began.

"Sorry?" he asked. "Don't be," he said when she nodded, her eyes filled with contrition and maybe a shimmer of tears. "As far as I'm concerned, I never heard it."

Without waiting for a reply, he went on to the house, but behind him, he heard the two women whispering, and he detected a note of surprise in their quiet voices.

He smiled. Maybe he could learn to be a nice guy after all. It wasn't nearly as painful as he'd thought it would be.

LOOKING AT HER WATCH, Paige wondered if Tucker had decided to write off both her and the therapy. Her face heated with shame just thinking of what she'd said about him. That he'd heard her say it only made it worse. In a way, she'd meant it to be a joke, yet it wasn't. He did have a lot of baggage, probably even more than what she was aware of. But, she reminded herself, she wasn't a mental health professional. She could only do what she'd been trained to do.

As the minutes ticked by, she wondered if she would even have the chance to help. It definitely appeared that Tucker wasn't going to show.

With a sigh, she left the darkened waiting room, where she'd been watching for Tucker, and walked to her office for her purse. She wouldn't worry. Tucker was a grown man. If he didn't want to carry through on the therapy, she couldn't make him.

But as she turned and started back, ready to leave, she didn't feel the relief she wanted to feel. Forcing her mind to the enjoyable things she could now do for the rest of the day, like taking a long soak in a bubble bath, watching a movie, maybe even reading something other than medical journals, she opened the door from the hallway and stepped into the waiting room—and collided with a large, hard body.

She let out a shriek, as a pair of strong arms held her in place. Why hadn't she locked the door before she went to get her purse? And then she realized who it was and that there was no reason to be frightened, except of her own reaction. Looking up, she saw a pair of deep brown eyes watching her in the semidarkness.

She heard an intake of breath, but didn't know if it was hers or his, and her heart seemed to stop beating.

"I was afraid you'd gone."

"You're late, Tucker," she said, jump-starting her heart and moving back, out of his arms to a safer place. "I wasn't sure you were coming. Not after—"

"The pickup was in use."

She nodded, and turned for the door. "You scared me to death out there," she said, as he followed her to the end of the hallway.

"You insulted me. I guess that makes us even."

Her heart sank as she flipped on the lights and they entered the room at the back of the clinic. "I thought we agreed it never happened."

When she pointed to the old examining table that had probably belonged to Doc Priller when he'd first begun his practice, Tucker moved and took a seat on it. "That's not quite what I said. But you were right."

Surprised, Paige looked at him and hoped he didn't notice her gasp when she saw that he was smiling. A real smile, not one of those polite ones she'd seen him offer to his family. A gorgeous smile that made him even more attractive. She silently reminded herself that he was a patient, and although she could enjoy working with a patient, getting involved in any way beyond the doctor-patient relationship was wrong. Very wrong.

"Let's put that behind us, shall we?" she asked in her most professional voice and moved to the table where he sat.

"Yeah. Sure."

"Go ahead and take off the brace," she told him and waited.

The afternoon had been unseasonably warm, and he wore a pair of cutoff sweatpants and a T-shirt. For a man who'd gone through what he had—nearly a year in captivity and countless time in hospitals—he was in remarkable physical condition. Muscles strained at the thin cotton of his T-shirt as he removed the brace. It wasn't easy to ignore, but she tried.

When the brace was off, she cleared her throat and concentrated on his scarred knee. "How have you been doing with the CPM? Any problems?"

"Some pain that first day," he answered, "but I expected it. Ice and the meds took care of it. Then lately some stiffness in the middle of the night, but I tried the ice, and it worked."

She nodded. "That can be expected. What about the exercises?"

"I've been doing them faithfully."

"Good. They help a lot. So let's get some measurements and see how far along you are."

"The machine read ninety degrees flexion," Tucker told her. "Pretty good, right?"

She smiled as she used the caliper to measure the bend in his knee. "Therapy is important in this type of injury. The surgery can't do everything." Just in case, she checked the number again. "Seventy-five degrees."

"But—"

"It's good, Tucker."

"It's not what the machine said."

She took a step back. "It happens. The machine's data isn't always completely accurate. Don't worry about it. You've definitely made some good progress."

"Not good enough."

"Much better than I expected," she assured him.

He moved to replace the brace. "Go ahead and say it. This isn't working."

"You're not hearing everything I'm saying. Tucker,

it'll take some time. Probably not a lot, but you're doing very well. It hasn't even been a week since you started the CPM. Some people wouldn't be where you are. And considering how long it's been since your surgery, it's wonderful progress. Don't give up. This *is* going to work."

He nodded, slowly. "All right. I'll give it a chance."

"Good," she replied, relieved.

"So what's next? More on the machine?"

"No, no more machine. I'll see you again on Friday, so bring it in then. I want you to keep doing the exercises until then and, if you feel up to it, you might try the high school weight room. Just don't overdo it."

"How will I know if I'm doing that?"

"Start anything new slowly. Any sudden, sharp pain is a sign to stop immediately. We'll see how far along you are and decide what the next step should be on Friday."

"Okay. Same time?"

"Let's make it for two-thirty. There's a game on Friday, so I'll need to be out of here early."

Tucker stood and leaned against the exam table, crossing his arms. "Must be nice to be able to take off when you want to."

Laughing, Paige shook her head. "Since I'm off to go to the school as the team doctor, it isn't like I'm taking time off. Besides, I'll make up for the missed time the following day."

"So the clinic is open on Saturdays."

"Half days, usually," she answered, moving to the cabinet to return the calipers. "Sometimes all day."

"And golf on Wednesday?"

"No," she answered, laughing again. "No golf for me, although my dad is a golfer."

"And a doctor?"

"Yes."

"My dad was a bull rider."

Paige had heard about the O'Brien family and how Brody O'Brien had been killed on the rodeo circuit when the hoof of a bull connected with his skull. The whole family had been involved in the rodeo, even Sally O'Brien, Tucker's Cherokee mother, and his sister, Nikki, too, when she was young. His brother, Tanner, had won the PRCA National Bronc Riding championship a few years ago, and Jules had told her about the injuries he'd endured throughout his career.

"You rode bulls, too, didn't you?" she asked.

"For a few years, before I joined the marines."

She was curious as to what led him to make that kind of change, but it was personal, and she wasn't going down that path. "So I'll see you Friday, all right?" she asked instead.

She couldn't read his expression as he pushed away from the table and started for the door. "Two-thirty?" he asked, when he made it to the door.

"Yes." She flipped off the light and as they exited the room she said, "I'll go with you to the front door. And now that I'm thinking about it, why don't you come around the back of the building then, instead of the front. The door is used by the staff only. If it isn't unlocked, just knock and I'll open it."

"Okay," he answered.

He continued to walk behind her, and she felt a little nervous, as if he might be watching her.

"One question, now that you brought up rodeo," he said.

She looked over her shoulder to see him frowning and wondered what he was thinking. The appointment hadn't started out well, had almost been a disaster when he'd thought he wasn't making progress, and now he appeared disturbed about something. "What's that?" she asked.

"It's about…"

He seemed to be struggling, but she was quiet, not wanting to push him.

"Horses. It's about horses," he said. "Riding horses."

The idea of him riding a horse with his leg and knee still weak made her cringe, especially because she guessed it was something he wanted to do. Why did he make things so difficult for her? It was as if she was destined to be his enemy, and she certainly didn't want it to be that way.

"I think it would be better if you wait a few weeks, Tucker," she answered honestly. "By then you should have full range of motion and there won't be any swelling or pain. That would be best, really."

"All right."

They'd reached the waiting room, and she flipped the switch, bathing the hallway behind them in darkness. "I hope you're not disappointed about the riding," she said, as they walked together toward the main door.

He was quiet as they stepped outside onto the sidewalk. She turned and locked the door, then tugged at it to make sure all was well.

"It's probably a good thing," he said from behind her.

She turned to see he'd started walking toward his pickup. "Why?"

Shrugging his shoulders, he stopped at the driver's side door of the truck. "It just is."

She sighed as she watched him open the door and climb inside. After he started the engine and backed out on the street, she finally started for her own car. "He's doing better," she whispered, hoping saying so would make it so. And she hoped that on Friday she'd get to see his smile again.

"HEY, DAD!"

Standing in the yard with a cup of coffee in his hands, while he enjoyed the early morning quiet, Tucker turned to see his son coming across the yard. "Leaving already?" he asked, as Shawn approached him. "I haven't seen Ryan yet."

"I have to pick him up today," Shawn explained. "His car is in the shop."

All Tucker could do was nod. He knew that when Shawn drove, it was usually the extra pickup truck, the one he'd been using and had planned to drive to his appointment with Paige later. Now he'd have to find another way to get there, without telling anyone where he was going or why.

"Are you coming to the game today?" Shawn asked.

Tucker realized he needed to start writing things down or keep a calendar or something. His memory wasn't as good as it should be. "Sure," he said, not wanting Shawn to know he'd forgotten. "What time did you say it started?"

"Four. Uncle Tanner and Jules will be there, so you can probably get a ride with them."

"Right." But Tucker couldn't tell his son that wouldn't

work. His appointment was at two-thirty. Somehow he'd find a way.

"I'll see you later then," Shawn said, turning away, then he stopped and looked back. "Is the knee brace helping?"

Tucker opened his mouth to ask how he knew, but instead answered. "I should've used it earlier. I didn't realize how much it would help."

"Maybe you can help me warm up again before the game?" When Tucker nodded, Shawn continued to the pickup. As he drove out of the driveway, he waved to Tucker.

Tucker returned the wave and watched the pickup disappear. With the usual pang of regret, he finished his coffee and then headed back to the house. Somehow he needed to get a ride into town early enough for his appointment. Either that or walk, and he didn't see that happening, even though he'd walked farther than that during his time in the marines.

He'd just sat down for lunch with the family when he remembered what Paige had told him about using the high school training room. He didn't know when it might be free, but he could at least find out when he might be able to use it. If he found a ride into Desperation, and that wasn't a sure thing.

Jules finally took her seat at the end of the table and looked down the length of it to Tanner. "Could you stop by the Chick-a-Lick while you're in town and pick up a cherry pie and an apple pie?"

"Can't we pick those up after the game?"

Jules shook her head. "They might be gone by then, and Darla said she'd only promise to keep them until two o'clock."

Surprised it was so easy, Tucker saw his chance. "Mind if I ride along?"

"Sure," Tanner answered, without looking up from his plate, "but you know you can always—" He looked up, smiled and shook his head. "I guess not today, since Shawn took it."

"It's too bad we didn't get Shawn that car for his birthday, but with the extra pickup—" Jules stopped suddenly and turned to Tucker, the hint of pink creeping across her face.

"It's okay," Tucker quickly told her. He felt bad enough about barging into their lives. They'd bent over backward, trying to make him comfortable, never prying, never asking questions. Jules had no reason to be embarrassed. "Besides," he continued, "it's time I got my own vehicle."

"There's no need," Tanner said. "Most of the time the pickup isn't used."

Tucker knew better than to argue with his older brother, so he didn't reply. But he would look into getting his own transportation. He didn't intend to stay at the Rocking O Ranch or even near Desperation, once Shawn graduated. Tucker saw even less reason to stay around than he had when he was fifteen. Maybe if he hadn't left then, things might be different now, but he'd made his choice and would live with it for the rest of his life.

But at least he didn't have to worry about getting to his appointment, and a little over an hour later, they were on their way into Desperation.

Tanner glanced at Tucker beside him in the truck. "You seem to be getting around better."

Tucker nodded. "I've been doing some work on my

knee," he admitted. "I hope you don't mind that I used your computer for a little research."

"No," Tanner replied. "You're welcome to use it whenever."

"Thanks."

Tanner pulled onto the main street and headed in the direction of the Chick-a-Lick Café. "Can I drop you off anyplace special?"

"No, the café is fine."

Tanner slid him another look, but said nothing as he pulled into a parking space in front of the café. Tucker barely waited for his brother to turn off the engine before he climbed out of the pickup.

"Are you going to make it to the game?" Tanner called after him.

"I'll be there. Thanks for the ride."

"Sure. Anytime."

Tucker could feel his brother watching him, but had purposely walked in the opposite direction of the doctor's office. The high school was only a couple of blocks in the direction he was going, so he decided to stop in and see when the weight room was available.

Walking up to the sprawling brick building, memories of the year he'd spent in it came rushing back. He'd hated school, wanting only to become a rodeo star. He smiled, but it was a sad smile. Quitting school and running off to join three older rodeo riders was the answer to all his problems—or at least that's what he'd thought. It was almost three years later that he realized what a bad decision he'd made, but by then he believed it was too late to go back home, even if he'd wanted to.

Avoiding the front door of the school, he skirted around the building to the back to slip inside the heavy doors. He remembered that the hall led to the boys' locker room, but once there, he realized he didn't know where the weight training room was. It had been far too many years since he'd been in the school. He should have expected changes, but he hadn't given it any thought.

Outside again, he looked around and realized there were two other buildings that hadn't been there when he was a student. Feeling totally lost, he glanced at his watch and decided to find out another time where he needed to go.

With time to waste, he stopped for a cold soda at the Sweet & Yummy Ice Cream Parlor in the historic opera house. From a table near the window, he could see the entrance to the clinic. When he saw the shades pulled, he knew the office staff would be leaving soon, and it was near time for his appointment with Paige. His leg was better, stronger and there were times when he didn't bother with his cane, although he still limped. He was ready to live his life, although he didn't know what kind or how.

After paying for his soda, he stepped out onto the sidewalk and started for the clinic. Out of the corner of his eye, he saw two figures moving down the street. Curious, he looked closer and was surprised.

He remembered Vern and Esther from his childhood. Now probably in their eighties, he couldn't believe that Esther was still chasing Vern. Rumor had it that they'd been sweethearts before Vern had joined the army, and when he returned, he wasn't interested in her anymore. Esther, however, hadn't lost interest, and it appeared she still hadn't.

Shaking his head, Tucker turned down the alleyway,

making sure no one was paying attention, and arrived at his destination.

"Right on time," Paige said as she opened the back door at his knock.

"I wasn't sure I was going to make it," he admitted, stepping inside the back hallway.

She led him into the now familiar large room and pointed to the tall examining table, as she always did. "Problems?"

"Lack of transportation, but I found a way into town."

"Where there's a will, there's a way, I guess."

Using the calipers, she measured the amount of flex in his knee. Thinking he'd been doing well, he was surprised when she looked up at him with a frown on her face. "What?" he asked.

She shook her head and moved away. "Nothing. I was expecting too much."

"What does that mean?"

She'd turned to replace the calipers on a countertop and looked over her shoulder. "There wasn't as much progress as I'd hoped there'd be, that's all."

He couldn't believe she was saying this. He'd worked hard and had hoped this would be the last appointment he'd have to have. Was it one more failure in his long list? He'd hoped he had left that road behind and was moving forward to something new. Something better. Apparently he wasn't.

Sliding down from the table, he stood straight. "Then I guess I'm wasting your time."

"No," she said, walking back to where he stood. "Sometimes therapy hits a point where there's little progression. I'm sure that's where we are with this now."

He shook his head, determined not to show his disappointment. He had thought and hoped— "I'm doing okay. There's no need for this anymore."

Without waiting for her to reply, he started for the door, but Paige's voice stopped him. "What is it with you, Tucker?" she asked. "You didn't want to do this to begin with, and now that I've proven to you that therapy can help, you've decided to *quit,* all because your progress has slowed a little?"

He refused to look at her and shrugged to show her he wasn't all that disappointed, even though he was. "I guess I owe you my thanks for getting me this far, but I can go it alone from here on out."

"Only you would think so," she replied, disgust in her voice. "There's more work to be done, Tucker."

"I'm fine." At least he would be.

"No, you aren't," she said, her voice cracking. "And I'm sure you won't do anything, once you walk out this door. I thought you were smarter than that. I guess I was wrong."

"What does that mean?"

"It means that nothing has changed. If you don't do the work needed now, a wheelchair could still be in your future."

Shaking his head, he continued to the door. "I'll be okay." But when he reached for the door handle, he stopped. Things weren't going his way, so he was going to quit? Except for his time in the marines, that's what he'd done all his life. When the going got rough, Tucker got going, but somewhere in a small, primitive prison in Somalia, he'd begun to see things in a different way.

He'd had time to look back at his life, and although he didn't make plans, knowing at that time that even the possibility of a future was dim, he realized that it was his choices that had gotten him where he was. Some choices had been good. Some hadn't.

And now it had come down to this. Sure, his leg was better, but it wasn't good. He couldn't deny that the improvement wasn't because of Paige. He'd practically forced her to help him, and maybe he owed her for that. Maybe he owed himself more than to quit and walk away.

"Okay," he said, turning back to look at her. "You win."

"No, you'll be the winner."

Her smile was slow. And sexy. And he wondered if she had any idea how sexy. Although he didn't want to admit it to himself, she'd become more than his doctor and therapist. Seeing her so often and working with her wasn't such a good idea. Had she been aware of this, too? Was that why she'd been so difficult about taking on his therapy?

But he couldn't let any of this stop him. He didn't want to end up in a wheelchair. No matter how much work it would take, he was going to see this through and hope he'd be rewarded with a leg that was strong and nearly normal.

When Paige finished giving him his therapy instructions for the next week, he helped her make sure doors were locked and lights were out, and then followed her outside the back door, where he'd come into the clinic.

"Where's your truck?" she asked, looking around the small parking lot at the back of the building.

He explained that he'd gotten a ride with Tanner and why, then told her goodbye and turned to walk away.

"Are you going to Shawn's game?" she asked.

He looked over his shoulder to see her standing by her car. "That's the plan."

"Come on," she said, unlocking and opening the car door. "I'll give you a ride."

He wasn't sure that was a good idea. "It's okay. The walk is good for me."

"And you'll be late, so get in."

Should he? He knew there would be questions, family asking what he was doing riding with the good doctor, and he hesitated.

"Tucker?"

"Yeah?" he asked, noticing she was now in the car.

"Just get in."

After hesitating another moment, he decided he'd deal with the questions, and he walked to the car, opened the door and climbed inside.

"I don't bite," she said as she started the engine.

"Never said you did." And he'd never tell her what kind of thoughts went through his mind, sitting in the confines of her car with her as she drove them to his son's game. Those thoughts were the kind he shouldn't be having.

Chapter Six

"How many more?" Paige asked from the hall.

At the reception desk, Cara turned to answer her. "Only one. Or two, depending on how you want to look at it."

Tired, Paige smiled anyway. Once this last appointment was over, everyone else would go home, and then Tucker would be here. They'd changed his appointments to one day a week and switched that day to Thursday, so they wouldn't have to work around baseball games and end-of-the-year school activities. "So how should I look at it?"

"It's the McPherson twins," Cara explained.

Paige looked out the open window in front of Cara to the waiting room. "If they're as healthy as I expect they are, it won't take long. Why don't you lock up? You might as well all go on home. Unless Kate mentioned concerns, this is a routine checkup, right?"

Cara scooted away from the desk. "Right. And thanks, Paige. It's been a long day for all of us. I'll tell the others they can leave."

Knowing it would be a few minutes before she would see Tyler and Travis McPherson, the twin sons of Dusty and Kate McPherson, Paige retreated to her tiny office.

She sat and leaned back in her chair, wishing the day was over, wishing the week was over. It seemed that during the past week, she'd seen every patient in Desperation. All she wanted to do now was go home, take a long, hot bubble bath and relax until it was time for bed. Unfortunately, that wasn't going to happen.

Minutes later, she was in the small examining room, checking the throat of nine-month-old Tyler, while his mother held a squirming Travis in her arms.

"They're healthy little guys," Paige told Kate when she was done with the exam. "They're definitely a handful, but you manage them so well."

"Thanks to Dusty," Kate replied, gathering her things. "He's a great dad and would have been here with me to help, but he had some errands to run. He'll be back in a few minutes, if he's not back already."

"He won't be able to get in," Paige told her, knowing the clinic had been locked when the staff had left.

"I know. Cara told me," Kate answered. "I called him and said to meet me outside. Next time we'll try to get an earlier appointment. I hate keeping you this late."

Knowing how Tucker didn't want anyone to know that he was getting therapy, Paige refrained from explaining why staying late wasn't a problem. "Don't worry about it. It isn't that late, and we're done, so there's no harm done." She picked up Tyler and held him, brushing her lips on his baby-soft cheek, then laughed when he wiggled in her arms. "They're both as healthy as can be," she said, giving him an extra hug.

"You should find some nice man to give you babies," Kate said, slipping the strap of the diaper bag over her shoulder as she got to her feet.

Paige sighed. "As if I have time for that."

"Which?" Kate asked. "A nice man or babies?"

"Both," Paige answered, laughing.

Kate followed her out the door and into the hallway. "You'd make a terrific mom. And there are a few eligible men in Desperation, if you know where to look."

"Where would that be?" Paige asked over her shoulder with a smile. "Lou's Place?"

"Hardly," Kate said with a chuckle. "But off the top of my head, I can think of at least one."

"And just who would that be?"

"Tucker O'Brien."

Paige stopped and turned, just as they stepped into the semidark waiting room. "Not you, too," she said with a sigh.

"But—"

"He's a patient." When she realized what she'd just said, Paige quickly corrected herself. "Or was, but could be again, I guess. And isn't that Dusty I see getting out of the pickup?"

Kate turned and looked out the door, the blinds half-pulled. "Yes, that's him," she replied, obviously forgetting about the subject of their conversation.

Paige unlocked the door, and Kate stepped outside, then turned back. "Thanks for everything, Paige. Now go home and relax. Get some rest. And think about what I said."

Paige laughed and nodded. "Yes to the first, but no to the second."

"You never know…"

"About what?" Dusty asked, walking up and taking Tyler from Paige.

"Never mind," Paige hurried to say, when Kate started to answer. Hoping to put an end to the subject, she bid them all goodbye and hurried back into the clinic, relocking the door behind her and making sure the blinds were closed all the way.

"They're nice people."

Paige jumped, but tried not to show she'd been startled. "They are," she replied, crossing the waiting room and walking to the doorway to the hall. She closed the door behind them and flipped on the hall light.

Tucker pushed away from the wall where he was leaning and followed her down the hallway. "My brother chose wisely when it came to picking a partner and best friend. I'm not surprised."

Paige didn't reply until they reached the room in the back. "You don't get along well with him, do you?"

Tucker, settling on the examining table, stopped and looked at her. "You noticed?"

"It's hard not to." She gathered his file and the calipers she needed to make the necessary measurements. "Having a sibling myself, I can understand being at odds sometimes. But your relationship with Tanner seems much deeper." She stopped, and shook her head. "But that's none of my business, so let's just get this done, shall we?"

"Now you sound like a doctor," Tucker answered as she took the needed measurements.

"Well, I am. Should I sound different?"

"It is after office hours."

The slightly seductive quality Paige heard in his suddenly soft voice tempted her to look up, but she refused to give in. "You're right," she said, hoping he didn't notice the husky quality in her own voice. "So why don't you tell me what it was like being a marine?"

After a short, uncomfortable silence, Tucker finally spoke. "You don't want to know."

Paige looked up and saw pain in his eyes. "I didn't mean your experience in Somalia," she said softly. "I meant as a marine in general. I've heard it's the toughest branch of the service. Why did you choose it?"

Looking away, he shrugged. "I heard some guys at a rodeo trying to pick a fight with a couple of the other bull riders. They said nobody was tougher than a marine."

"So is it true?"

His smile was wry, and his chuckle was soft. "I suppose it is. Boot camp definitely is the worst of the lot."

"But you made it through it," she pointed out.

"I did. But just getting there was tough. If it hadn't been for Grandmother Ayita, I wouldn't have been able to join."

"How's that?"

"I quit school when I was fifteen. I needed a diploma. She knew a man who could help get me one."

"I've heard Nikki speak of her," Paige told him. "So you made it through boot camp. Did you like life as a marine?"

"I did," he said, nodding. "I'd still be active, if it wasn't for…" He stopped and stared at her. "Why are you asking me these questions?"

It wasn't hard to miss the anger in his voice. She knew it would be wise to stop. She didn't have the training to be doing this. "I'm curious," she answered. "I haven't known a marine—at least not that I'm aware of—and I've always been curious."

"Be curious with someone else."

Seeing the look of pain on his face and hearing the anger in his voice, she decided not to ask him more. But she'd gotten him to talk a little about his past, and she considered that a major step. At least he'd opened up, if only a little.

"So how's my knee now?" Tucker asked in the silence, the anger still evident in his voice.

She moved away, swallowing a sigh of frustration. "It's good. Better than good, actually."

"But we aren't done, are we?"

She tried for a smile and hoped he didn't notice that it was forced. "No, but we're getting close."

"Then I'll see you next week," he said, moving off the table.

"It won't be long," she told him as he walked past her as if she wasn't there. "The more you work at it, the stronger your leg will be."

"I've stopped taking the pain pills."

"That's good." But she was disappointed that he wouldn't look at her. Talking about the past had brought out the worst in him. Was it because it was a time he didn't want to revisit? She couldn't blame him, when it came to his last experience as a marine. He seemed to be angry at the world, but she wondered if it was himself he was angry with.

"Same time next week?"

She looked up to see him standing in the doorway. "Yes, same time."

He left the room, and she listened to his footsteps as he walked down the hall and then out the door in back. There was so much to like about Tucker, if only he'd let people get closer. But she knew that getting closer to him wouldn't be good for her. She had no idea what his plans were, but she could sense that he wasn't a man who would ever settle down. He'd obviously seen the world—some of the worst parts of it—and had experiences that had left him with emotional scars. He wasn't the kind of man she needed, no matter what Kate or Jules or anyone might think. She just wanted to help him.

Or at least that's what she told herself as she turned out the light.

JUST AS BEFORE, it was as if he'd stepped back in time. The barn was quiet, except for an occasional swish of a tail, a soft whinny or a muffled clip-clop of a hoof. He'd been thinking even more since his last appointment about doing what he hadn't done for almost twenty years, and now Tucker was ready to give it a try. But which horse should he choose?

If he'd been thinking, if he'd planned this, he should've asked which horse belonged to which family member. He didn't want to saddle and climb on someone else's mount, but he hadn't asked, and besides, there were extras. There always were. The O'Briens were generous with their stock and kept extras for guests and visitors. But who would he have asked? Jules? She would've been concerned if he was able to ride. He couldn't have answered her. He didn't know the answer—one of the reasons he wanted to try to ride without anyone knowing.

"That buckskin there might be a good one."

He turned at the sound of Rowdy's voice. "You should've been in Special Forces," he told the man, "the way you're able to sneak up on people."

Rowdy snorted. "I don't sneak. I just mind my own

business and keep my mouth shut, until I find it necessary to say something."

Tucker couldn't argue with that. Rowdy had been at the Rocking O for as long as Tucker could remember. He knew his father had hired him as his first ranch hand when his father had purchased the land, then had later made the man the ranch foreman. Rowdy knew more about the ranch than anyone. And, if truth were told, probably about the O'Brien family, too.

"I've kind of had my eye on the sorrel," Tucker admitted.

"Good choice, but a little more on the frisky side. Think you can handle him?"

Tucker considered the question. "I don't know."

Rowdy nodded and his smile was slow and knowing. "Give him a try. You'll do fine."

There was no argument from Tucker. He'd thought he'd never walk again without pain, and now the little pain he had was manageable. He wasn't completely clean of the meds yet, but he was getting there. Riding was another goal he was working toward. He might be rusty at it, but he was learning to give himself a chance.

Rowdy turned to walk away, but stopped and looked back. "Need any help saddling?"

"I think I can remember how," Tucker answered, smiling as he thought of all the times he'd saddled a horse when he was young. "I guess trying will tell the tale."

Rowdy's expression didn't change. "Yep. Extra saddles and bridles are in the tack room, along with saddle blankets in the cupboard. If you need me, give me a shout."

"Thanks," Tucker said, as he watched Rowdy leave the barn.

Once he'd gathered the equipment he needed, Tucker started saddling the horse he'd chosen to ride. Only once did he hesitate, but it wasn't because he'd forgotten, it was because he realized he'd done it all to that point without giving it much thought.

It was when he went to mount that he had a problem. Although his left leg was stronger than it had been even a few weeks ago, he found it difficult and a bit painful to reach his left foot into the stirrup, not to mention the leg being strong enough to boost him upward to swing his right leg over the saddle. It took several tries, and he nearly quit, but he finally succeeded and started his ride, in spite of the new pain he was feeling.

His discomfort was quickly forgotten as he revisited the ranch he remembered from his childhood. There was no doubt that Tanner had worked hard to make the Rocking O a success, and Tucker marveled that his older brother could do it, while still keeping active in rodeo.

But once the coveted gold buckle was his, Tanner had chosen retirement, had married and then had begun a family to carry on the O'Brien name. Tucker had to admit his brother had more perseverance than he'd ever had himself. The only thing they seemed to share was their last name, and he wondered if Tanner had ever regretted even that.

Tucker didn't realize how much time had gone by as he'd ridden over the ranch land, seeing again the hills and valleys, the creeks and pastures that had fascinated him so many years ago. If it hadn't been for his father dying on the rodeo circuit, maybe things would have been different, but that was something none of them would ever know. And Tucker had never regretted becoming a marine, even when he'd believed he would never survive his capture.

A sudden rumble in his stomach finally prompted him to check his watch. Realizing he'd missed lunch and could easily miss his weekly appointment with Paige, he urged his horse back to the barn, where he found Rowdy and Tanner saddling their horses.

"Thank God," Tanner said, as Tucker rode into the yard.

Tucker urged the sorrel through the open gate and into the corral, where he dismounted, wincing at the pain in his knee. "Did you think I got lost?" he asked, looking from one man to the other and suddenly feeling like he was eight years old.

"You were gone a long while," Rowdy said, "and, well..."

"Better safe than sorry," Tanner said, and headed for the barn, leading his horse.

"I lost track of time," he answered with a shrug. "It's been a long time."

"Everything's okay, right?" Tanner asked, when Tucker led his horse into the barn.

"My knee's a little sore," Tucker admitted. If he'd been truthful, it was more than sore, and he wished he'd had enough sense to know it wouldn't be easy getting on and off. But he'd sure know better the next time. Right now, he needed to clean up and see Paige. He quickly corrected his thought. He wasn't going to see her, at least not in the way most people would think. No, not at all. He just needed his knee checked. And he had a bad feeling she wasn't going to be happy with him.

It wasn't long before he was proven right.

"You're limping," Paige said as Tucker walked in the back door of the clinic.

"It's nothing."

"Really?" she asked, following him to into the big room.

He didn't bother to even glance at her. "I'm fine."

"I'll be the one to determine that."

Not wanting to talk about how foolish he'd been, he wasn't in the mood to argue. "I took one of the horses out for a ride, that's all."

Without saying anything, she waited for him to take his place on the table. When he pulled up the leg of the sweatpants he'd worn, she let out what could only be called a disgusted sigh. "Your knee is badly swollen."

"I'll be all right," he insisted, even though his knee hurt like hell and he wasn't convinced he hadn't done some serious damage.

"This time," she said.

When she looked at him, their gazes locked. Her eyes reflected her concern, and he felt bad for causing it. He knew he should've checked with her first about the riding, but he'd honestly thought there wouldn't be a problem. Would she believe him if he told her that? He doubted it.

"Tucker, I know how much you want to be normal, for your leg to work like it did before you were injured. And it can. But you have to take the right steps and do the right things to make that happen. Pushing yourself beyond what's safe could do more damage, and that could mean damage that might not heal completely."

A large lump had formed in his throat, and all he could do was nod his understanding. He didn't know why he felt this way. He usually didn't feel this kind of emotion. Whatever was causing this, she cared. About him.

"So what can I do?" he asked and was relieved when she finally smiled.

"You've been working with the recumbent bike at the high school?" When he nodded, she continued. "Keep using it and keep icing. If anything you do causes sharp pain, stop immediately. And I'm serious about that. I also think it's time to move on to the last list of exercises."

The last list. That sounded good to him. He knew it wasn't over yet, but it was getting close, and except for what he'd done today, he'd been doing pretty good.

"One more thing," she said.

"What's that?"

"Start walking. It's good for overall conditioning."

"And here I was thinking of getting myself a car," he joked.

But instead of laughing or even a smile, she continued. "No jogging. Absolutely none. Walking only."

"Okay." He'd done enough five- and ten-mile runs in the marines that a leisurely walk sounded good. But Paige seemed distracted, and he didn't know how to ask if it was something he'd done. His little riding experience hadn't turned out as well as he'd thought it would, and he wondered if she was angry with him. And why should he care? But watching her walk away, he couldn't drag his gaze from the sway of her hips, the shape of her long legs, or just the sight of her.

He was in trouble.

PAIGE PLANTED HER HANDS on her hips and looked up at the ceiling of the cavernous building. The barn, which had once housed livestock after it was built in the early 1800s, had withstood the ravages of time as well if not better than the old Colonel's house had. Now a community room for the use of not only those who lived at the Commune, but also anyone needing the space, it was currently in the process of being turned into a glittering fairyland for Desperation High School's junior-senior prom that night. Thanks to Hettie Racine Lambert, the great-great-granddaughter of Colonel George Ravenel, the prom would not be held in the school gymnasium as it had been for years, and the students were thrilled.

"How many strings of white lights do we have?" Paige asked.

"There's ten of the regular size here," Jules answered, "and six of those tiny ones."

"And those are the regular ones around the perimeter?"

"We have two more regular strands left."

Paige turned to look at her friend. "How opposed do you think they'd be to having one of the big, shiny disco balls in the center?"

Jules laughed. "Other than thinking it's cheesy? I think they'll get used to it and like it."

"I do, too," Paige agreed. "So let's try putting one up in the center, then string those small lights out from that to the corners of the room."

"Good idea, but where will we find a disco ball?"

Paige frowned and shrugged. "I don't know."

Kate joined them, carrying a large box of votive candles. "I do. Or at least I have an idea where one might be found." Her smile was Cheshire catlike as the other two waited. "The Blue Barn."

Paige shook her head, thinking of the notorious

honky-tonk located not far out of town. "Oh, I don't know—"

"Oh, pooh," Kate said, setting the box on the floor. "Dusty and I had our wedding dance there, and I seem to remember seeing one of those balls in a storage area when we were checking out the place during our wedding planning. I'll just have Dusty go and find out."

Paige still wasn't convinced, but she liked the idea of using it to have the lights dancing around the room. "If you think so."

"I'll get him on it right now," Kate announced and walked away.

Jules looked at her watch. "I really should run up to the Commune and check on Wyoming. Hettie volunteered to watch him while we decorated. Why don't you take a break, too?"

Taking one more look at the room and imagining how it would look when they were done, Paige nodded. "I wouldn't mind a breath of fresh air."

"You go on," Jules said. "I'll let the others know we'll be gone for about fifteen minutes."

Happy to have a few minutes to herself, Paige stepped outside the building into the beautiful early May afternoon. Since moving to Desperation almost a year and a half earlier, she'd learned that Oklahoma weather could be fickle, especially in late spring. But there were no indications of storms for the weekend, and she was happy the prom-goers could enjoy their special evening and not worry about the weather.

Although she'd been to the Commune to visit friends and patients before, she'd never really looked around the grounds surrounding it. With a few minutes to wander, she crossed to the back of the huge, ancient barn, and found herself in an old orchard. It was obvious it wasn't in use anymore, but the trees were in bloom, and she walked farther into the orchard, amazed at the natural beauty around her.

"They're apple trees."

Paige spun around at the sound of Tucker's voice, and her heart raced. "They're beautiful," she answered, suddenly feeling a little breathless.

"The story goes that Colonel Ravenel had the orchard put in for his wife, Anne," he explained, walking toward her. "The family kept it up for a couple of generations, but after a while, it was pretty much let go. I used to play here when I was a little boy. Most of us did. Apples make great ammunition, especially when they're rotten."

Paige laughed, imagining Tucker with his friends, pelting each other with soft, icky apples. "I'm sure they do." She looked up at the nearest tree. "I seem to remember hearing Hettie say she'd like to see it restored."

"It would take some work," he said with a shrug, "that's for sure. But what are you doing, roaming around out here?"

She took a few steps and began a leisurely walk through the trees. "I'm helping with the decorations for prom."

"That's where I was headed," he said, following a little behind her. "Jules said there'd be plenty of work for the men, what with all the hanging of this and that. Not that I know anything about proms."

"You never went to one?"

"Proms weren't high on my list."

He'd moved to walk beside her and she stopped, turning to him. "You know, that's too bad. Proms are like an American rite of passage."

"I suppose. So were you prom queen or whatever?"

"Me?" Paige asked, laughing. "Not hardly."

"Why not?"

She could've sworn he was closer, but she hadn't seen him move. Shoving the thought aside, she answered. "I was a gangly teenager with my nose in a book."

"But you did go to a prom."

"Yes," she said, and quickly changed the subject. "What else did you do here when you were young?"

He looked up at the tree they were standing under, and as she looked up to see what had caught his attention, he pressed his lips to hers. So taken by surprise she didn't know how to respond, she didn't try to push him away, not even when he pulled her into his arms. His wide chest was solid. Strong. And she felt a rush go through her as a strange calm settled around her. It seemed an eternity before he stepped away, leaving her wanting, but knowing she shouldn't.

"Wh-what—" she stuttered, not sure what she should say.

He pointed up, and she tilted her head back to look in the tree.

"Mistletoe," he said.

"You're kidding." She'd heard some strange stories, but this one beat all. And then she saw it, the green, glossy leaves tangled within the branches of the apple tree.

"It's Oklahoma's state flower."

"It's not really a flower," she answered, as her head began to clear. "It's a parasite."

"A quasiparasite, but it is the state flower." His smile

was slow and so sexy her breath caught, and then he spoke. "You asked what else we used to do out here when we were young. Now you know."

Her laugh began like a tiny bubble in her chest, and then erupted. "You brought girls out here and kissed them, using mistletoe as the excuse. How awful of you!"

He shrugged, and his smile grew wider. "They didn't mind it."

And Paige had to admit she didn't mind it, either, except that it had left her with feelings she couldn't name or explain. And it was wrong. Over the few weeks they'd worked together on his therapy, she'd tried not to admit how strong her attraction to him had become. If she'd been any other woman, all would be well. But she was a doctor. He was, in a way, her patient, and she was teetering on the breach of unethical behavior.

"I guess I should get back," she said, needing to get away from him. His answer was a nod, and he said nothing. She tried to smile, but her worry made it hard. She wasn't sure what she should do. If she stopped helping with his therapy, refusing to work any longer with him, would he quit? He'd come so far, she didn't want to see that happen. But if she did continue to help, she would have to guard her feelings and make sure nothing else ever happened again.

Chapter Seven

Tucker waited on the porch for Shawn. When his son stepped outside the house, Tucker joined him. "Ready?"

"Ready."

Before the two of them reached the steps, Tanner appeared in the doorway. "Where are you two headed?"

Tucker felt the old resentment sneak through him. Tanner playing father. First to him, then to Shawn. But Shawn was eighteen now. If he wanted to go somewhere with his father, what business was it of Tanner's?

"We're headed to the city to find Dad a car," Shawn announced and smiled at Tucker.

"Or truck," Tucker added. He noticed Tanner's eyebrows had gone up.

"If that's what you want, Tucker," Tanner told him. "Good luck. By the way, Davis Auto in the city is one of the best, we've found. Gene will cut you a good deal."

Tucker nodded. "I'll keep that in mind."

Once they were in the pickup and on their way, Shawn turned to Tucker. "Any idea what you're looking for?"

Tucker thought of Paige's brother's fancy sports car. It might be nice, but it wasn't something he'd be comfortable with. "I don't know," he answered as honestly as he could. "Maybe I'll know it when I see it."

"A pickup?" Shawn asked. "You mentioned that. Do you think you'll be hauling stuff, like at the Rocking O?"

Tucker wondered if Shawn was trying to find out if he planned to stay at the ranch.

"No, no pickup," he answered. "And I'm not sure about a car, either."

"Then what about an SUV?"

Tucker considered it. "Well, that would solve the need of having a bit of hauling space."

"Sure, plenty of room for stuff or people. And if you're smart and can afford it, you'll go green."

"Green?"

"Yeah, like with a hybrid or a crossover."

Tucker suddenly wished he'd done some research before just taking off with nothing specific in mind. He'd been out of the mainstream of life for so long, he wasn't familiar with all the newer things going on. "Green meaning ecological, you mean?"

"That's it!"

Tucker hoped Shawn knew more about all this than he did. But then it didn't really matter, as long as they could find a vehicle to get him wherever he would be going in a few weeks. That's all he really cared about when it came to transportation.

"I heard you helped with the prom decorations," Shawn said a few minutes later.

"Not really," Tucker answered. "By the time I got there, most everything was done." He didn't want his son to know that he'd purposely gotten there late. After surprising Paige with a kiss he hadn't planned, he'd

decided it'd be better if he left. It had started out inno-
cent enough, but he knew by Paige's reaction that he'd
stepped over the line. Way over.

"I'm glad you brought your date by for pictures," he
said, changing the subject. "She's a pretty girl."

"Laney and I have been friends since grade school,"
Shawn answered, chuckling. "If someone had told me
even two years ago that I'd take her to our senior prom,
I'd have laughed."

"I guess people change, but if you're around them
every day, you don't see it."

"Maybe." Shawn was quiet for a moment. "Your leg
is better, isn't it?"

Tucker glanced at him, then returned his attention
to the road ahead. "It's definitely stronger than it was
when I came here."

"You've been seeing the doctor, then," Shawn said,
his voice quiet. "Dr. Miles."

The last thing Tucker wanted to do was to tell everyone what he was doing. His biggest fear had been
that he'd let his family down and wouldn't succeed with
the therapy. But things were turning out a lot different
than he'd thought they might. Maybe it was okay if he
admitted that Paige was helping.

"She's been overseeing my physical therapy, yes," he
answered.

"She's nice."

"Yes."

"And you kind of like her, don't you?"

For a second, Tucker held his breath. He already
knew Jules liked trying her hand at matchmaking, but
his son? "Like you said, she's nice," he answered. "She
didn't have to help me, but she did."

"Then why haven't you asked her out?"

Tucker took his eyes off the road to stare at his son. "A date?"

"Sure," Shawn answered. "Why not? I mean, she's nice. You like her."

For a brief second, Tucker wondered if taking her to dinner would be a good way to thank her for her help. It was quickly replaced by the memory of the kiss in the old orchard, and he knew that dinner or anything else would be a bad idea. He'd come to like her too much. Way too much, and it was time to put some solid space between them, before he started thinking things he shouldn't. He didn't have any business getting involved with anyone.

"Just think about it, okay?" Shawn asked.

Tucker wished he could stop thinking about it, but it wasn't easy, even as they looked at vehicles and eventually bought one at the dealership Tanner had suggested. When he could keep his mind off Paige, it was a miracle.

When he arrived at his next appointment a few days later, he sensed things were a bit strained between them, and he mentally kicked himself for it.

"Did you hear that I finally got a car?" he asked her as he settled on the examining table. "Shawn helped me pick it out. It's a hybrid SUV."

"I'm glad you have your own transportation. How's your leg and knee feeling?" she asked, approaching him with the calipers.

"Good," he answered, noticing she hadn't looked directly at him since he'd first walked into the clinic.

"Let's get the measurements then." She quickly finished the task and stepped back. "You're doing some walking, right?"

"That's what you told me to do last week. Is something wrong?"

"No, nothing," she said, finally meeting his gaze for a brief moment. "Are you still using your cane?"

"Sometimes," he admitted. "It was so much a part of me—"

"It's time to get rid of it," she said quickly. "You're still depending on it and really don't need it."

Tucker stared at her. "Okay, if you say so."

She nodded. "Keep up the exercises, and I'll see you next week at the same time."

When she turned and walked to the door, then gave him a polite smile, he wasn't sure what to think. It had only been a kiss. Under the mistletoe. It wasn't as if he'd had his hands all over her or— He shook his head as he moved off the table. She was angry, and maybe she had a right to be. He'd probably been out of line. It had been so long since he'd been that close to a woman— But he'd learned his lesson, and he sure wasn't going to do it again.

"Next week, then," he said, and left, feeling like a kid who'd been caught with his hand in the cookie jar.

PAIGE STEPPED INSIDE the big round-topped metal building at the Rocking O Ranch where the senior class party was being held. She'd been tempted to make an excuse and stay home, but she didn't want to do that to her friends. The O'Briens had been more than kind since she'd arrived in Desperation, and she owed them and others more than avoiding an event that certainly wouldn't kill her to attend.

"There you are," Jules called to her. "We saved you a seat."

"In the back of the building?" Paige teased when she reached her friend. "Just what kind of chaperone are you?"

"The kind who knows her place," Jules answered with a wink.

Paige looked around the dim building, where crepe paper streamers and balloons decorated the walls and the metal girders of the ceiling. "Where is everyone?"

"The men are out tending the barbecue pit. Trish is keeping watch over the punch and soft drinks. Bridey is keeping the salad bar filled, and Kate is inside putting the last touches on the dessert."

"So what can I do?" Paige asked, feeling badly that she hadn't arrived earlier. "If I'd known there was so much to be done—"

"Don't worry about it," Jules told her and pointed to the chair next to her. "There are always more people than we need at these kind of things."

Paige nodded as the rest of the O'Briens and their friends began drifting to the table.

Dusty was the first to reach one of the empty chairs and pretended to collapse in it. "I really thought I loved smoking meat, but now that I've smoked enough for a herd of elephants, I think I'll retire."

"They're growing kids," Trish said, as she joined them. "But I agree, at least as far as the potato salad goes. If I have to peel one more potato, the peeler may become designated as a weapon."

Paige was aware when Tucker was the last of the group to return. She'd noticed he rarely seemed comfortable when his family—especially Tanner—was around. Tucker was so different than she was. Although she and Garrett lived a long way from their parents, who lived in a suburb of Chicago, they were a close family. She was sorry Tucker hadn't had the same kind of experience.

A bright bluish white light swung through the building toward the table where the adults were sitting, and Paige shaded her eyes with her hand, trying to see where the light was coming from.

Jules leaned closer. "One of the boys borrowed a few of the spotlights from the school theater. I guess they're putting us in the spot, so to speak, although I don't know why."

"I'm sure we'll know soon," Paige said, as she watched one of the students step up onto a makeshift platform, holding a microphone.

"Yes, those are our chaperones," the young man announced as the spotlight swept back and forth across the table in the back. "Hi, there, O'Briens and friends."

Nearly everyone at the table answered.

"We have you in the spotlight," he continued, "because we want to thank you for sponsoring this party tonight, our class's last high school party, and for giving us a place to have it." He waited until the applause from the young people died down. "We weren't sure what we could do for a special thank-you that you'd remember, but one of the parents came up with an idea. We hope you like it."

Strains of an old slow dance song came from the enormous speakers at the corners of the platform, while another young man took the microphone from the first one. "We had some trouble finding the right music, but we hope you'll all enjoy dancing to this one, because, well, this one's for you."

As the spotlight dimmed, Tanner stood and helped Jules from her chair, and she turned to the others at the table. "This is for everyone, not just the two of us. Dusty? You and Kate come on. Trish, Paige, don't be shy."

Paige watched as they all slowly began to drift to the dance floor, while trying to ignore that she and Tucker were the only ones left at the table. Wishing she could disappear, she moved to leave the table, thinking a trip to refill her glass of soda was the best idea, but she wasn't able to complete her escape.

"Dad," Shawn said, approaching their table, "it's time to try a new exercise. I'm sure Dr. Paige won't mind helping you with this one, will you, Dr. Paige?"

Paige opened her mouth to beg off, but knew it would do no good. Shawn wasn't going to let her escape, nor was he going to let his father get away with not dancing.

"Paige?" Tucker asked, standing and holding out his hand to her. "I don't see any way we can get out of this, so we might as well make the best of it."

Nodding, she took his hand. "You're right."

He led her to the edge of what had become the dance floor, and then turned her in his arms. "I promise I'll behave," he said with a wry smile.

Unsure of how to reply, she said nothing.

Taking a deep breath, he let it out slowly. "I might as well admit that it's been a long time, so you'll have to bear with me."

"For me, too," Paige admitted, without looking up and into his eyes.

They moved together, swaying to the soft, melodic and well-known song, and it wasn't long before Paige relaxed and began to enjoy the dance.

"He's a good kid," Tucker said. "I guess I have my brother to thank for that. I don't suppose it was easy for him, but he's not the kind of man to turn his back on family."

Paige looked at him and saw that he was watching Shawn, who stood with the girl he'd been seeing and several other couples. The group seemed to enjoy watching the chaperones dance, and she smiled. When she glanced up at Tucker, love and pride shined in his eyes, but she also saw something else.

"What is it, Tucker?" she asked, without thinking.

His smile was sad as he continued to watch the group, and his voice was soft when he answered. "I'm proud of some of the things I've done, especially after I joined the marines. But when I see Shawn and realize how much I missed, not only of his life, but of having and doing the things most teenagers experience, I sometimes wish I could redo my life after I left here."

"I can understand how you might feel," she answered.

He turned to look at her. "Can you?"

"I think everyone can, at least about some things."

"I suppose."

But she suspected he didn't understand, so she did what she could to explain. "We make choices every day, every minute of every day. Sometimes they're small, like choosing to get out of bed…or not, and sometimes they're big and life-changing. Sometimes we believe they're right, and they can be." She thought of her own life, of her teen years when she'd begun the big focus on a medical career. Looking back, she realized now how that choice had left her with little time for her friends, who finally drifted away, and even less time for boyfriends.

"The past is behind us," she thought aloud. "What we need to remember is that we can make the best of the present and the future, if we try."

The music began to fade, and the dancers around them were slowing. Tucker slowly came to a stop, one hand still around her waist, the other holding her hand, as he looked out over the crowd in the room. "Maybe. I just wish I knew how."

Before she could answer, a loud blast of music filled the room, and the two of them followed the others who were hurrying back to the table.

"That was nice of them," Jules said, taking her seat at the table.

"It was," Kate agreed as she settled on her own chair. "You know, I don't believe Dusty and I have danced since our wedding."

Dusty leaned forward as he helped her scoot her chair closer to the table. "Is that a hint?"

Kate laughed. "Only if you think it should be."

Talk turned to the past, a time before Paige had arrived in town, and she listened with interest, as she always did. And she noticed that Tucker, too, seemed to be listening. But every now and then, he'd look toward the teenagers with that same sad, wistful look on his face. And she didn't know how she could help him begin to look to the future, instead of dwelling on the mistakes of the past.

TUCKER LEANED his folded arms against the corral fence, the past reaching out to grab him. Throughout his adult life, he'd tried to forget everything that had happened before he'd joined the marines. He never succeeded. And now it all poured over him as memories swirled in his mind.

As far back as he could remember he'd wanted to be a bull rider like his dad. Nothing and no one could stop his determination. When he was ten, they owned two bulls. He'd managed a few times to climb onto Wooly Bully, the tamer of the two, but it was Macho Man, a mean crossbreed of unknown lineage, that he wanted to ride. He refused to give up and finally managed to coax and lead the bull into the corral from the pasture, then proceeded to jump on the animal's back from the top rail of the fence. The ride, what there was of it, was something he'd never forget. So was the paddling he'd gotten from his dad, who just happened to be home between rodeos.

But he'd also seen the pride in his father's eyes that he'd been smart enough and brave enough to do the deed. Even Tanner, at thirteen, had been impressed, whispering congratulations as their dad walked toward the house.

But when Brody died at a far-away rodeo, life at the Rocking O changed. Looking back, he realized how much they all had changed, for better and for worse.

When the sound of a vehicle could be heard coming up the drive, he was pulled from his memories and turned to see who it was. The thirty-year-old restored Mustang meant Shawn's friend Ryan had stopped by.

"Hey, Mr. O'Brien," Ryan called to him, waving, as he walked up to the house.

Shoving away from the fence, Tucker greeted him, and then walked around the house to the back patio.

He always enjoyed spending a few minutes there in the morning, before checking to see if he could help with chores. Sometimes Jules would join him, but today he could hear her behind him in the house, talking to Shawn and Ryan.

"There's orange juice, if you'd like some, Ryan," Tucker heard her say. "Shawn, sit down and stop pacing. Your uncle will be here in a minute."

"Yeah, Shawn," Ryan said. "I'm sure he'll say it'll be okay."

"Don't bet on," Shawn replied. "You know how he's always been. If it wasn't for Jules— Everything was fine, and now it's like it was before."

"You know how your uncle feels about parties that aren't chaperoned, Shawn," Jules said. "It isn't that he doesn't—"

"It's the rule," Tanner said, walking into the room.

Tucker shook his head. How many times had he heard those same words? And they always meant an end to the discussion.

"It's a special occasion," Shawn pointed out. "An after-graduation party."

"With drinking and all the rest?" Tanner said. "No, you don't have to answer that. I already know."

"But I don't do that!"

Tucker got to his feet and turned toward the house. Opening the door, he stepped inside and looked around. Jules, usually the calm one, glanced at him with a worried frown. Tanner wore his "what I say goes" look, while Shawn had crossed his arms, his stubborn expression saying it all. Ryan looked as if he was ready to bolt, but afraid he'd be caught in the act.

"What's this about a party?" Tucker asked.

Shawn turned to look at Tanner, then focused on Tucker. "A bunch of us—most of the class—decided to have a party out at Parson's Creek after graduation."

"There'll be drinking and carousing," Tanner pointed out again. "I don't imagine many of the parents are going to allow this."

"So it all comes down to what everybody else thinks and does?" Tucker asked.

Tanner's frown deepened. "No, it doesn't. It has to do with being smart."

"Are you saying Shawn can't be trusted?"

"No, and he knows that."

"Then why not let him go?"

"Because it's a *rule*."

Sadness slid through Tucker. "Yeah, I remember those. You know, I've heard guys say the marines are tough, but you've got even them beat, Tanner. You always did."

"You went wild after Dad died," Tanner replied. "You don't have any idea what it was like to have the responsibility of everything, including a little brother. You never had any responsibility."

Tucker couldn't deny the truth, but anger churned inside of him. He'd resented Tanner in the past for trying to be his father, and he resented him now for trying to be Shawn's. Even worse, Tanner *had* been Shawn's father, and it was Tucker's own fault.

"He's eighteen," Tucker said, trying his best to diffuse his anger. "He's old enough—by law—to make his own decisions." He turned to Shawn. "Go to the party, but use your common sense. Drinking can get you in trouble. All kinds of trouble. Sometimes trouble you don't even know about," he added, thinking of how he'd become a father.

Tanner took a step closer to Tucker. "You can't do this. You can't walk into my house and cross the rules I've set."

"He's my son," Tucker said simply.

"And I raised him," Tanner shot back, "while you were out playing at the rodeo, so irresponsible you didn't even know you had a son."

The words felt like knives, cutting through him, and Tucker turned on his heel and shoved out the door. By the time he got to his SUV, his emotions were churning so hard, he couldn't think straight.

As he drove out of the yard, fingers clenching the steering wheel in a death grip as he headed for anywhere but the Rocking O, he couldn't deny that Tanner had spoken the truth. He *had* been irresponsible, but it had been Tanner who had made him that way.

He was in Desperation before he even knew where he was going, and pulled into the high school parking lot, sending gravel flying as he came to a stop. He hadn't been this angry since the day he'd left the ranch when he was fifteen, determined to show his older brother that he was a man.

Only he hadn't been a man then. He'd been a kid and had felt the death of his father deep in his soul, but he hadn't allowed himself to acknowledge or show it. He'd been a kid whose mother had cared more about rodeo than her two sons and left them behind. Or so he'd been told at the time.

Grabbing the gym bag he'd left in the backseat, he slammed the car door behind him and strode to the back door of the school. It was Saturday, and Jim Perkins would probably be around, doing paperwork that never got done during the week.

Tucker found the coach in the weight room, putting away a stack of clean towels. "Mind if I work out a little?" Tucker asked.

"Go ahead," Perkins answered with a nod in the direction of the equipment. "I've got a family thing to go to, so lock up when you're done." He turned and studied Tucker. "You look like you need to burn off some energy or something, Tucker. Feel free to use the whirlpool when you're done. It can do wonders for those times when you'd like to snap someone's head off."

Tucker thanked him and changed into his workout clothes. As he settled on the weight bench, he squeezed his eyes tightly shut. He hated fighting with Tanner, always had. But his brother had to learn that he wasn't always right.

Tucker hadn't shed a tear since his dad had told him his mama had left them. Not when he learned his dad had been killed by a bull, not when his unit had been hit by marauders and he and Smithson had been wounded and left to die. Not even when he held Smithson as he drew his last breath. But at that moment, his eyes filled with hot tears, and all he could do was hope he could stay around until Shawn's graduation.

Chapter Eight

The tires on Paige's car crunched on the gravel of the empty school parking lot as she pulled in and parked. After turning off the engine, she leaned her head back against the seat of her car and sighed.

She hadn't been sleeping well, and after a long Saturday morning at the clinic, all she wanted to do was go home and crawl into bed. Her friends were expecting her to join them at Kate's later that night, and if she wanted to be something more than a walking zombie, she knew she needed a nap. But she'd told the coach she'd be by with the new workout sheets.

Making herself move, she reached for the papers on the seat next to her and slowly climbed out of her car. She knew why she wasn't sleeping well, but she didn't want to think about it. Doing that would only make it harder to forget, meaning she'd lose even more sleep. As she walked toward the building where the weight training room was located, she did what she always did when she was stressed and tried to envision a clear mountain stream, shutting out the kiss with Tucker under the mistletoe, and then the dance they'd shared. If only she could wipe out the memory of his hand curved around her waist, and his other hand holding hers.

Unfortunately for her, the trick was beginning to wear off, and she shook her head, sighing again at her own weakness.

She'd expected to find the coach in the training room, and called out his name as she walked through the door. Getting no reply, she searched for him in his office, but found it as empty and silent as the hallway had been. Thinking he might be putting away equipment from the game the day before, she looked for him first in the locker room, and then in the weight room, without success. When she heard sounds in the whirlpool room, she headed there, expecting to find him stacking towels.

But it wasn't the football coach she found. It was Tucker.

She froze inside the doorway, her gaze riveted on his wet, muscled arms stretched out along the tub rim. His head was leaned back, and he looked perfectly at peace, the opposite of how she was suddenly feeling. His eyes were closed, and his dark, wet lashes rested on high cheekbones, as steam drifted above the water to curl his dark hair and caress his bare shoulders and chest, glistening from the water swirling around him. His lips curved in a whisper of a smile of silent contentment.

She didn't know how long she stood there, drinking in the sight of such perfection, but it couldn't have been long. When she jumped and let out a slight squeak at the sound of the heavy door behind her closing, reverberating through the room, it was too late to make an escape.

Tucker's eyes opened, and she knew the moment he saw her. He smiled.

She opened her mouth, but words escaped her. No

simple hello, no apology came forth, just a slight intake of air as she watched him move to sit forward.

Reality hitting her was like a slap in the face. "I—I was looking for Coach," she explained, and then realized that her voice was breathy, as if she'd been running. Her heart thudded in her chest and she swore it was probably loud enough that he could hear it.

"He was here earlier," Tucker replied, "but he said something about having to go to some family thing." Reaching for a towel on the small stool beside the tub, he grinned. "Better close your eyes, Doc. Guys tend to do this kind of thing in the all-together, and I'm no exception."

Without thinking, she did as he suggested and listened to the splash of water as he moved. Certain he must be standing now, she was almost tempted to peek, but a quick reminder that she'd seen more than her share of men's naked bodies kept her from it.

"You can open them now."

She did. He was walking toward her, a towel knotted at his waist, another in his hand as he mopped at his damp hair. This was not the time to let her fantasies run away with her.

But before she could speak, she had to clear her throat. "Is your, uh, knee giving your trouble?"

He stopped less than a foot in front of her, his gaze penetrating. He shook his head. "No trouble."

Her lips trembled when she smiled. "Good."

When she took a deep breath to steady herself, his scent invaded her. Heat radiated from him, and she knew it wasn't only because of the warm whirlpool. She felt her own heat, burning like a flash fire through her.

A whisper in her mind cautioned her. Warned her.

But it was drowned out by her need, shouting loud and clear. And she no longer craved sleep. She craved something else, something completely forbidden.

She didn't notice he'd stepped closer until he spoke, his voice a raspy whisper. "I want you, Paige."

Her mind warred with her body, but the heat won as she reached out and tentatively ran the tip of her finger down the middle of his chest. The contact was like lightning, and his sharp intake of air proved he felt the jolt of it, too.

Her legs nearly gave out, but she managed to remain standing. What was next, she wondered? Should she leave? Or should she—

"This isn't fair." His voice was husky. Rough.

She closed her eyes, trying to think of a reply, but it was as if she'd just finished off a gallon of cheap wine. Her mind was not cooperating, but, oh, her body was, and completely out of her control.

A gentle touch at the buttons on the front of her loose, cotton knit dress forced her to open her eyes, but it was an effort. It was as if she was drifting slowly through a dream. Had she fallen asleep in her car in the parking lot and was now dreaming?

Opening her eyes, she looked directly into his. If this was a dream, she hoped nothing would awaken her from it. If it wasn't—

But she didn't finish the thought, as he slipped each of the small buttons of her dress through the openings, never taking his eyes from hers. She wasn't sure if she was still breathing, when he slowly eased her dress off her shoulders and then let it drop to the floor.

A shiver of heat and need raced through her when his lips touched the soft spot between her neck and her shoulder, and she sunk her teeth into her lip to keep from groaning out loud. Her head was spinning so fast that she leaned forward and was stopped by his rock-hard chest against her bare breasts. When had…?

The thought evaporated as he put his arms around her and pulled her closer. Common sense tried to intervene, but something deep inside overruled it, and she willingly raised her lips for the kiss she so needed.

TUCKER KNEW WHAT THEY were doing was probably wrong, but he didn't care. He hadn't been able to stop thinking about Paige since he'd met her, even though he'd been determined not to like her. Ignoring the attraction hadn't worked, and it had only gotten worse. He'd wanted her long before he'd kissed her in the old orchard, but each time those feelings tried to surface, he denied them. What was happening now was nothing more than a natural progression of desire. He'd fought it long enough, and this time he wasn't going to ignore it and pretend otherwise.

He moved to slip an arm under her legs and lifted her into his arms. Never giving a thought to the knee and leg that had led him to meet the woman he was carrying, he looked around the room. A weight room wasn't the ideal place to make love to a woman, but there'd been worse. And then he remembered the tiny room where the wrestling equipment was stored. It was as prefect as they would get. And it had a door that would lock… just in case.

"Where—?"

"Shh," he answered, adding a quick kiss. "Trust me on this." At the equipment room, he twisted the doorknob, and the door swung open. As he'd hoped, there was a tall pile of wrestling mats in the corner.

"This is cozy," she whispered, with a note of humor.

Easing her to her feet, he chuckled. "Better than the floor."

"Or a weight bench," she said, nodding to one in the opposite corner.

He reached for several towels that were stacked on a high shelf and arranged them on top of the stack of mats. When he finished, he slowly lowered the two of them to the mat.

He'd noticed when she first walked in, even in the dim lights of the whirlpool room, that she'd worn her dark hair down, and now he lifted one springy curl and watched it wrap itself around his finger. Burying his face in her fragrant hair, he breathed in the scent of it. Wanting to ignore the urgency he was feeling, he slowly moved her beneath him, where he touched his lips to her throat, feeling the throbbing of her pulse.

He felt her fingertips caressing his back, and then her hands slid along his sides to his hips as she raised her own to press closer. When she pulled his lips to hers, kissing him with an intensity that lit an internal fire that burned deep, he stopped thinking.

Slipping his hands under her hips, he lifted them and slowly—to the point of his own pain—entered her. She raised her hips higher, driving him deeper, and sighed.

Burying himself in her was like diving into a warm pool, the water swirling around all of him, and he groaned. She moved beneath him, setting the rhythm, and he followed. Their hands caressed each other, their lips met time and again, touching and tasting, as they delighted in each other.

He wanted these moments to last, but his stamina wasn't what it once had been. Neither, he realized, was his control when he took her over the edge. Watching her face, feeling her around him, he couldn't do anything but follow.

The reality of where they were returned too quickly, and he soon slipped out of the room to gather her things. When he returned, she'd wrapped a towel around herself and was sitting in the middle of the mats, her legs folded beneath her, her brows knit in what he suspected was worry.

"I think—"

"Don't," he said. "This wasn't something to think about, it was something to experience."

"But—"

He shook his head as he placed her clothes next to her. "Let it be. For now, anyway. Just don't—"

"What?"

He wanted to tell her not to have any regrets. But he was afraid she might not understand if he did. Instead of answering, he shook his head again and slipped out of the room.

He'd gone too far, taken advantage of her, when he knew there couldn't be a second time. He was leaving in a few weeks. He couldn't allow himself to be involved with her. She'd only get hurt.

As he turned off the whirlpool and dressed, he attempted to put their lovemaking aside in his mind, but images of Paige kept creeping back to tease him into believing there might be more for them. He knew better. He'd always failed at relationships, from his family to friends to women. This time would be no different. If he was going to succeed at any relationship, it had to be the one with his son. Maybe someday, in the future, when things were different and he was—

He swallowed hard and shook his head. He was only fooling himself, and he vowed not to do the same to Paige. He just didn't know how to tell her.

When she emerged from the equipment room, fully dressed and buttoned up, he instinctively moved toward her, but the smile she gave him wasn't one of a woman who'd just experienced making love, and he stopped.

She didn't look directly at him when she asked, "Is your knee all right?"

"My—?" He stared at her, stunned at her attitude, as if nothing had happened. At the same time, he knew it was best for him and apparently for her, too. Something in his chest felt heavy, but he ignored it and answered her question. "It's fine."

Nodding, she walked to the door, but hesitated when she reached it. She turned for a moment, as if she would say something, then opened the door and slipped outside.

He didn't know how long he stood there, watching the closed door. Too long, he told himself when he realized he hadn't moved. Turning, he noticed a pile of papers on a chair and picked them up. There was a note attached for the coach and signed by Paige. He left the papers in the office and looked around to make sure nothing else had been left behind, especially anything of Paige's. After making sure the main door was locked, he got in his SUV and headed back to the ranch, hoping to put the afternoon behind him. But doing that proved more difficult than he'd imagined. Just one more reason to get away from Desperation, he said to himself in the confines of his vehicle, refusing to acknowledge the sadness he felt.

PAIGE SAT IN HER CAR in her driveway, her forehead pressed to the steering wheel. Had she completely lost her mind?

Tears stung her eyes when she thought again about the afternoon with Tucker, and she sniffed them back. No matter how she really felt about it, she couldn't ever admit to having enjoyed it. In fact, she couldn't admit that it had ever even happened. He was her patient! What she had done was not only inappropriate, but also a breach of ethics.

She doubted Tucker was even aware that they'd stepped over the bounds into a very dangerous area. Not that she thought he would bring charges. After all, he was the one who'd—

The tap on her window brought a shriek from her and she sat up immediately to find Garrett motioning for her to roll down her window. Taking a deep breath, she did.

"Are you okay?" he asked, his eyes filled with concern.

"Just…I'm just tired," she answered, grabbing her purse and reaching for the door handle. "We were really busy today."

He stepped back as she pushed the door open. "Some days are," he agreed and turned for the house.

She joined him and felt another concerned glance as they both stepped onto the porch. Still worried, she tried to cover it with a smile.

"I know you're tired," he commented after he'd

opened the door and she'd walked inside, "but if that's the best smile you have, you're in trouble."

"Funny." Dropping her purse on the back of the sofa, she headed down the hall to the bathroom, where she planned to splash some cool water on her face. That or drown herself. She hadn't decided.

"If you're that tired," he called down the hallway, "why don't you take one of your two-hour bubble baths and go to bed?"

It sounded heavenly, and she was very tempted, until she remembered she was expected at Kate's for the evening. Without realizing it, she groaned.

"It can't be *that* bad," Garrett called to her.

If only you knew, she thought. But that could be disastrous. Usually having a brother who was an attorney was a good thing. In this case, it might be just the opposite. When she was in the right, it was all good. Only this time she wasn't. Not that she'd have Garrett handle any medical case for her. That wasn't his area of law. But he'd always been a good sounding board for general questions.

Her feet and her heart felt like lead as she returned to the living room. "Girls' night out," she announced, trying her best to sound chipper. At least it was at Kate's and she didn't have to worry about Tucker passing by as she said something she shouldn't.

"So call and tell them you can't make it," he suggested. "They'll understand, right?"

Nodding, she considered it. Jules, Kate and Trish understood how stressful her job could sometimes be. She couldn't ask for a better staff, and she blessed Doc Priller for his wisdom in hiring the people he'd hired. But what it all came down to, now that she was the doctor, was that the clinic was her. That's the way people in Desperation—or anywhere else—saw it.

And she'd foolishly risked everything she'd worked for since she was in high school. Even worse, she couldn't talk with anyone about it. Not Jules, Kate or Trish. Not Garrett. And Tucker would never understand. He was accustomed to taking risks.

Realizing she was on the verge of panic, she closed her eyes and took a deep breath, then slowly released it. She wasn't one to jump into bed with any man. But Tucker wasn't any man. He wasn't the type to report her. Maybe she was hoping for too much. Disregarding what had happened between them, she was feeling things she shouldn't. Just how much of a fool was she for falling for him, when she had no idea if he was capable of the same thing?

Feeling only slightly better now, she knew deep down that spending time with her friends would make her feel normal. With them, she wasn't a doctor or the town caretaker, she was a woman. If she didn't spend the evening with them today, it might be a month before they were together again. She needed them.

"I think I should go," she finally stated.

Garrett smiled. "Whatever you think is best."

"What about you?" she asked. Her brother was as busy as she was, much of the time.

Shrugging, he sat on the sofa and spread his arms along the back, looking completely relaxed. "I think I'll go down to Lou's Place and grab a bite. There's always a good crowd on Saturday nights, and I haven't been there for a while."

She felt better and decided to put what had happened

that afternoon behind her, at least for the evening. "Then we're both guaranteed a good time."

After a quick shower, she dried her hair and found something comfortable to wear, including a new pair of sandals she'd forgotten she'd bought one weekend while shopping in Oklahoma City with her friends. At Kate's, Trish noticed them immediately.

Leaning forward in her chair on the patio, Trish pointed to Paige's shoes. "Are they as comfy as we thought they'd be?"

"Light as a feather," Paige replied, sticking her feet out and wiggling them.

"And so pretty, too," Jules remarked. "I knew I should have bought the blue pair."

"Maybe we should plan a trip into the city just for that," Kate suggested, passing out glasses of lemonade to the others.

Jules sighed as she took the glass Kate offered. "If only there was time. With graduation only ten days away—"

"So soon?" Trish cried, and then shook her head. "I can't believe Shawn is graduating and will be gone soon, off on his trip with Ryan."

"Not much of a trip," Jules said, laughing.

"Where is it again that they're going?" Paige asked. "He told me, but sometimes there's so much going on with patients, I forget what's happening with friends." Not to mention that she'd been so focused on Shawn's dad... The thought made her lean back in her chair and wish she could disappear. Thank goodness no one could read her mind.

"They're headed to California first," Jules answered.

"I'm not sure anymore what their agenda is after that, but they're expected in Arizona by the middle of June."

Paige suddenly remembered what Shawn had told her. "That's right. They have that summer internship."

Jules nodded. "Once it's over, there'll be less than a week before college classes start."

"He's going to OU?"

"For a year. Both he and Ryan decided to stick closer to home, at least for now. I think Shawn's especially glad he did, now that Tucker is back."

At the mention of Tucker's name, images of him in the whirlpool, his skin damp from the water and heat, of him standing in front of her, a towel slung low on his hips, drifted through her mind, and she pressed her lips together. Would this be her punishment for overstepping the bounds? To have these images and memories invading her mind when she least expected or needed them? She was a grown woman, not a hormone-driven sixteen-year-old girl! But, oh, how little shocks had skipped through her when he'd touched her, and she'd needed—

"...coconut lemon cake."

Paige blinked, and her surroundings returned to normal. Maybe staying home and enjoying that long bath would have been a better choice.

"Sounds heavenly," Trish said, sighing. She turned to Jules. "Have you heard from Nikki? She'll be home for graduation, won't she?"

"She called just before I left home," Jules answered. "They're leaving Mac's parents' home tomorrow and hope to be here in a couple of days."

Trish's eyes twinkled with mischief when she smiled.

"They've been gone almost two months. That's one long honeymoon."

They all laughed, and Jules shook her head. "If it hadn't been for the opportunity to visit so many EAP facilities around the country, she never would've agreed to leave."

"Does she have her certification?" Kate asked.

Jules nodded and smiled. "It didn't take her long to get it. They had a wonderful time, but she's looking forward to getting home, not only to be back at the Bent Tree with the boys, but to have the chance to spend some time with Tucker. They barely had a chance to speak when he showed up at her wedding reception."

Paige remembered the day well. Nikki and Mac were getting ready to leave on their honeymoon, when Tucker came walking up the O'Briens' drive, after having disappeared almost twenty years before. Or so she'd heard later, because as soon as the family realized he was there, chaos had erupted. And now he was causing chaos in her life, even though he didn't mean to, she was sure.

When dinner was over, the four of them began clearing the table. While the others chatted about their children, Paige's thoughts wandered to earlier that day, even though she tried hard to concentrate on what the others were saying. Guilt and worry invaded her thoughts as memories of earlier that afternoon kept playing through her mind.

How had she allowed herself to fall for him? And she had. Hard. No matter how wrong she knew it was, it had happened, and now she had to find a way to deal with the fallout. His injuries were healing, and his knee and leg were stronger. It might be wise if she called a halt to her part in his physical therapy. Except to make sure that he didn't reinjure anything, she wasn't needed. He was able to do the necessary exercises on his own. He'd come a long way in the weeks since he'd first come to her office. He could do it on his own. Maybe that would be the best thing for both of them.

"You're awfully quiet tonight," Jules said. Kate and Trish had returned to the patio, leaving Paige and Jules to follow. "Is something bothering you?"

When she felt her cheeks heat, Paige turned away, hoping her friend didn't notice. "I'm a little tired, that's all. Some days are busier than others." Thank goodness Jules had no idea just how busy the day had been and what had gone on.

"I suspect you've been working some extra hours, too."

Paige turned back, wondering what Jules might be talking about. "Am I supposed to know what that cryptic remark means?" she asked, adding a smile.

"We haven't missed the fact that a month ago Tucker could barely walk, even with the help of a cane," Jules answered simply. "And now only someone who knew about his injuries would guess what it was like before. I know he isn't driving to the VA for therapy."

Cornered, Paige wasn't sure what to say, and so she shrugged and remained silent.

"You're not going to admit you've been helping him, are you?" Jules asked.

"I'm not. Not officially."

Jules smiled. "I see. This is off the books, right?"

Paige had a feeling she might as well be as honest as possible. "I've been overseeing his therapy, suggesting exercises and monitoring his progress, nothing more." Except for falling for him and wishing she could do more.

But it wasn't his physical injuries she worried most about now. It was his mental state. He still held himself away from others, even her, in spite of what had taken place between them that afternoon. She was too close to him emotionally and her heart, unfortunately, was involved, so she didn't believe she was the person to help. Besides, she didn't have the training for it. Jules, on the other hand, did.

"Do you know anything about what happened in Somalia?" she asked Jules.

Leaning back against the sink, Jules crossed her arms and shook her head. "He still keeps all that bottled up. It's not healthy. Has he told you anything?"

"No. Getting him physically healthy was my goal."

"Just how did you talk him into the therapy? He was totally against it when any of us brought it up."

"He came to me after I'd tried and failed to talk him into getting some help with his knee." The surprise on Jules's face prompted Paige to explain what had happened before Shawn's baseball game, when Tucker had nearly fallen.

"Shawn mentioned something, but didn't go into details. He worries about his dad. I'm not surprised he was the one who made the difference to Tucker," Jules admitted. "If it wasn't for Shawn…"

"I know," Paige agreed, nodding, but considering everything, she didn't know of any way now that she could help him.

Chapter Nine

"There you are."

Tucker looked toward the big double doors at the far end of the barn and saw his sister walking toward him. Nikki and their grandmother had been the only family members he'd seen after he'd left the Rocking O, and Nikki hadn't even known who he was.

From what he'd learned, Nikki had arrived at the Rocking O the previous fall, looking for a job at the Bent Tree Boys Ranch, Jules's ranch for disadvantaged boys. Nikki had been certain Tanner was her brother, but even after Jules hired her, she didn't reveal who she really was. When Tanner learned her identity, he wasn't willing to accept her, but as he discovered secrets neither he nor Tucker had been aware of when they were boys, he soon welcomed her into the family.

Smiling at him, she came to a stop near where Tucker sat with an old saddle from his childhood in his lap. "Still wearing that frown, I see."

Ignoring her jab, he turned to look at her. In the briefest of time they'd had before she and her new husband left on their honeymoon, he'd felt a bond with her that he couldn't explain. "Were the boys happy to see you?"

"Oh, they tried not to show it," she answered, laughing, "but they didn't succeed very well."

"What about Kirby?" Tucker asked. Kirby was the young boy she and her new husband—the head wrangler of the boys' ranch—were adopting. "How's he doing?"

"Mac's with him, explaining how we're going to be a real family now, with a house and everything."

"He's a great kid."

"True," she said with a sassy smile. "But why are you just sitting there? Saddle up and let's go for a ride." When he hesitated, she grabbed his arm and pulled. "Come on, it'll do us both good."

Realizing she wasn't going to take no for an answer, he got to his feet. Fifteen minutes later, they rode their saddled horses out of the corral and toward the pastures.

"You know," she said, as they left the ranch proper behind, "it's really going to be nice to have the whole O'Brien clan here together. I never dreamed it would be possible."

But Tucker didn't want to talk. Not about the future. Not about the present. And definitely not about the past. Not now. He also didn't want to tell her that he didn't plan on staying after Shawn's graduation. "I'm happy it's working out for you."

Riding next to him, she tipped her head to the side and studied him. "That's a strange thing to say. It's working out for all of us, isn't it?" When he didn't answer, she moved her horse closer. "What's bothering you, Tucker? Can't you see how great everything is going to be?"

He stared at the leather reins in his hand. "Is it?"

"What do you mean? After all these years, you're home again. Can't you see how much that means to all of us?"

He shook his head, unable to put his feelings into words. When he'd called his grandmother from the VA hospital, she'd told him he was the father of an eighteen-year-old boy, and he'd worked harder, making plans to leave as soon as possible. Later she'd called to say that Nikki was also at the Rocking O and getting married in only a few days. He'd gone not only to meet his son, but also to wish her well and let his family know that he was still around. He'd given in to his family's requests to stay, so he could get to know his son, but that was it.

And then Paige had come along and healed his body, changing everything. Now he might actually be able to do something with his life. But what?

"Tucker?" Nikki said, jerking him from his thoughts. "Talk to me."

"I don't know," he answered, more to himself than her. "I don't know that I want to stay here. I never planned to."

He could feel her staring at him when she replied, and wished he hadn't even hinted that he might be going away.

"But there's no reason you can't stay, is there?" she asked.

He wasn't sure. "Tanner and I don't get along," he admitted. "We probably never will, so staying might not be such a good idea."

"But—"

"And that's my fault."

"I don't see what makes it your fault."

He turned his head to look at her. "I left. Just like Sally."

"Sounds like a cop-out to me," she answered. "You can't blame her for everything."

"I don't! I blame myself."

They rode along in silence for some time, before Nikki spoke again. "Race you to the creek."

He barely had time to react before she was yards ahead of him. Urging his horse into a gallop, he took off after her, thinking about the mother he barely remembered. He'd overheard people whisper about her and her wanderlust, and he realized that he had the same. Throughout his life, he'd never been able to stay in one place. He'd never had a relationship that had lasted any length of time and had learned to avoid them.

"I've failed, Nikki," he admitted, when he finally caught up with her at the creek, where she'd already dismounted. "With my family and everyone I've ever been close to." And now he'd fail with Paige, too.

"That's in the past, Tucker," she told him. She waited until he was off his own horse and had looped the reins over a nearby bush to continue. "It's time to stop looking backward, enjoy the now and look forward to a better future."

"Is it?" he asked, hope fading as he thought about what his future would be. If he'd ever had what was needed to be part of a relationship, including a family, he'd lost it, long ago.

Nikki reached out and put her hand on his shoulder. "You have a son," she reminded him. "Now that he's found you, I'm sure he wants you to be a part of his life."

Tucker tried to think of what a future might be, but

Shawn was grown and no longer needed him. Tanner had provided the guidance Shawn had needed when he was young. Tanner had been the father Tucker should have been. He was tempted to tell Nikki that he was leaving, but he was certain she'd tell Jules or Tanner, so he didn't say anything.

Nikki pulled her hand away and sighed. "I wish I'd known you when we were young."

"I do, too. I guess I made the wrong choices."

"Sometimes we do, but that's how we learn."

"I suppose some people can," Tucker agreed. "But things are different with me."

Sighing again, Nikki walked to her horse and mounted. "Only if you want them to be."

He untied his own horse and climbed onto the saddle. He didn't want to disappoint her, but he didn't know what else to do. She hadn't lived his life. She hadn't had to make the choices he'd made. She hadn't experienced what he had.

In a week, Shawn would graduate. A few days after that, he and Ryan would leave for the coast and then their internship in Arizona. Tucker had missed all of his son's childhood except for these last few weeks. There wasn't a way to recapture any of it. He only hoped Shawn would understand.

He returned to the barn and discovered Nikki had already put her horse away. But the things she'd said echoed in his mind. Was it possible to correct the wrongs so many years later? Could he turn those bad choices around, forget what needed to be forgotten and make his life something to be proud of?

Could his family forgive him?

Could he forgive himself?

BEING STUBBORN COULD sometimes be a good thing, Paige decided. She'd been determined to put "the incident at the high school," as she now referred to it, out of her mind. Anytime her thoughts wandered to the "incident," she quickly turned them to something else. It was working. Most of the time.

Closing the door behind her after another long day at the clinic, she kicked off her shoes, crossed the living room to the sofa and collapsed. She was exhausted. The problem with not thinking about the "incident" was that all this ignoring wore her out. And if she was really honest with herself, the more she tried not to think of it, the more those tiny memories—the sensation of his touch, of how his kisses took her breath away—battered at her. She might be occasionally winning the battles, but she was afraid she was losing the war. And it had only been four days!

The house was blessedly quiet. Garrett would be attending the city council meeting later and would go straight from his office to there, so she had the house to herself until late. Leaning her head back, she sighed. Maybe it wouldn't hurt to stop fighting for just a little while. Maybe if she let herself fully experience those feelings from the "incident," they wouldn't try to keep creeping into her thoughts.

She was mentally reliving the moments before Tucker had picked her up and taken her to the wrestling storage room, when she was jerked back into the present by the sound of her doorbell ringing.

"It's probably for the best," she muttered as she shoved herself from the sofa and walked to the door. Opening it, she was surprised to find Shawn standing on the other side.

"Jules asked me to return your punch bowl," he said. "And thank you for letting us use it at the party."

Paige took the heavy, cut-glass punch bowl from him and stepped aside. "Come on in and make yourself comfortable, if you have some time. I've been wanting to hear about the trip you and Ryan are taking."

"Thanks."

Paige slipped into the kitchen and quickly put the punch bowl away in the cabinet, then returned to the living room and settled on one of the chairs across from the sofa where Shawn sat. "It won't be long now," she said, smiling. "Less than a week! Are you excited?"

Shawn nodded. "Sometimes it doesn't seem like it's possible. It's like I remember my first day of kindergarten, and how Uncle Tanner took me to my classroom. When I think about it, it's almost like it was only a couple of years ago."

"Time flies when you're having a good time," Paige said, "or so I heard when I was young."

"But so much has happened lately, and it's all been good," Shawn continued. "That's what's really mind-blowing for me. Like my dad coming back."

Paige wasn't sure what to say. She hadn't given a lot of thought to Shawn and his reaction to all that had happened in the past couple of months, except to think that there must have been some changes made in his life that no one had expected. As far as Tucker was concerned, she sensed that his whole life had changed when he met his son, and she could only imagine how difficult it was for him. And for Shawn now, too.

Shawn leaned forward. "I asked Jules if I could return the punch bowl, because I wanted to thank you for helping my dad."

Paige wondered if Jules had said something to the boy. "You don't need to thank me."

"I know you helped him."

"Did he tell you that?" she asked, wondering what else Shawn might have learned.

He shook his head and leaned back again. "No, I just guessed. After he hurt his leg so bad before that ball game when he was helping me warm up, I asked him if there was something he could do, and he admitted there was. Then I made him promise he'd do it."

Paige couldn't hide her smile. "And you assumed he came to me."

"I didn't think he'd ever do it, even when he'd promised, but he did, and look at him now."

"I'm glad I could help," she told him, meaning it. She felt good about it, too.

"He's a good guy," Shawn said. "I wish he'd been around when I was growing up. Not that Uncle Tanner wasn't good to me," he hurried to say.

"I know your dad wishes the same thing. It was because of you that he came to me for help," she explained.

Shawn sighed and shook his head. "He's stubborn, like all the O'Briens. I just hope he stays around. I know he and Uncle Tanner have some issues...."

"Is everything going okay?" she asked.

Smiling, Shawn shrugged. "Jules says it's going about as well as it can, considering."

Paige wasn't sure what he meant. "Considering?"

"Yeah. Uncle Tanner and Dad had a—" He chuckled and ducked his head. "Jules calls it a difference of opinion, but it sounded more like an argument Saturday."

Just the mention of the day made Paige's cheeks heat. "This past Saturday?"

"Yeah. I never should've mentioned the party some of the kids are having after graduation. That's what started it."

And just what, she wondered, did that have to do with what happened between her and Tucker later? She could only imagine what might have gone on with Tanner. She hadn't forgotten how Tucker had reacted to the mention of his family the first time he'd come to the clinic. "I'm sure they'll work things out," she told Shawn. "Give it a little time. Sometimes siblings don't always get along. Garrett used to make my life miserable when we were kids, but I wouldn't trade him for anything now."

Shawn stared at his hands, now clasped between his knees. "I guess it's just different for them, what with my dad running off like he did, and then my mom leaving me with Uncle Tanner. I was a handful for a while, I know. We all have Jules to thank for making things better. She's really special." He slowly looked up. "It'd be nice if my dad had somebody special."

Paige instinctively knew she needed to be careful. "Special?"

"Yeah. If you and he—"

She didn't miss the hopeful gleam in Shawn's eyes, and she didn't know what to say to him. "Well, thanks for thinking of me," she said, trying to make light of it, "but I'm not so sure that's the best idea." Especially, she thought, since she'd fallen in love with the man. She really had no idea what was in Tucker's mind or what his plans were. She hoped he was staying in Desperation, but he'd never really talked to her about it, and she'd never felt she should ask. Just why was that?

"I think it's a great idea," Shawn said.

Paige stared at him. The glint in his eyes that she suspected was a bit of the devil, as Bridey would say, made it difficult to know if he was serious. She hoped he wasn't. She'd already made it clear to Jules—at the price of a huge embarrassment—that matchmaking wasn't needed, and she didn't need Shawn trying his hand at it.

"You still haven't told me about your trip and your internship," she said, changing the subject.

The nudge finally took, and Shawn began to describe in detail how he and Ryan had been planning a trip to Los Angeles since they were in middle school. Paige listened, but she wasn't able to put thoughts of Tucker and Shawn's hint out of her mind. She really needed to find a way to put what had happened with Tucker behind her. Deep in her heart she wished it meant something important was happening between them, but she tried hard not to believe it did. And that she and Tucker would be the only ones to ever know about it. Even more, she prayed there would be no surprises. Not only had she overstepped the bounds of ethics, but they also hadn't used protection.

SEATED AT A big round table, the wooden top worn and scarred from years of use, Tucker looked around the noisy tavern, remembering the time he'd gone in to find his dad and to take him home. It was a period not long before Brody left for the rodeo circuit to look for Sally, when Brody had taken to drinking more than he should. Tucker remembered how angry his dad had been, but Brody had eventually given in to Tucker's pleadings and gone home. Tucker knew he couldn't have been more than six, but very little had changed in the tavern, except that it was called Lou's Place now.

Country music played on the jukebox that still sat next to the door, and several men, both young and old, were playing a round of pool nearby. For a weeknight, the place was doing a brisk business. Tanner had explained when they'd arrived that part of the reason for the crowd was because of the barbecue beef sandwiches that Dusty's wife made and were sold at the tavern.

Tucker was finally comfortable around his older brother's friends. Once he could remember their names, it hadn't taken long to get to know them and like them. Dusty, tipped back in his chair, was discussing the merits of handmade saddles with Mac, Nikki's new husband, while Tanner listened.

The sudden loud crack of a cue ball hitting another ball behind him at the pool table caused Tucker to grab the edge of the table to keep from diving for cover. He hoped nobody noticed. Loud, sharp noises like that always put him on his guard. They reminded him of sniper shots, one of the many things from the last few years he wished he could get over and forget, but hadn't.

Around the pool table, laughter followed and then someone shouted. "Hey, we could use some beer over here, honey, if you'd just move that sweet butt of yours."

Tucker frowned and glanced at the man in the blue shirt who'd said it. From what he could tell the last thing the guy needed was more to drink. But it wasn't his place to say so.

Morgan, seated across the table, leaned forward.

"Kind of noisy tonight," he said, glancing in the direction of the pool table.

"I guess it can get that way," Tucker replied.

"So what are your plans for the summer?"

Not yet ready to let his family know he didn't plan to settle at the Rocking O or anywhere near Desperation, Tucker shrugged. "I haven't really made any plans yet."

"I don't blame you. Take it easy while you can. Real life sets in soon enough." He looked up in the direction of the door and waved. "Over here, Garrett," he called out.

Tucker looked over his shoulder to see Paige's brother walking toward them. Not that he was surprised. Although this was the first time he'd joined this group of men at the tavern, he knew they got together when time allowed. He hadn't planned to be there, but Tanner and Dusty had both insisted. Now that he was here, and except for the occasional crack of a cue ball, he was beginning to relax and feel glad he'd agreed to come.

Garrett took the empty chair between Morgan and Tucker, and greeted everyone as the waitress approached.

"How's my favorite cowboy tonight?" she asked, setting a cup of black coffee in front of Garrett.

Knowing Garrett wasn't anything close to a cowboy, Tucker watched, curious, as Garrett looked up at the blonde woman. "Hungry," he answered, grinning.

"I'll have it for you in just a minute," she said.

"Wait," he said, before she turned to walk away. "Tucker, how about you? Kate's sandwiches are the best."

"Sure," Tucker answered, not that he was hungry. "Thanks."

"Make that two," Garrett told the waitress.

She nodded and smiled at both of them, and then moved away. But before she could get past the pool table, the guy who'd yelled for the beer grabbed her. Sensing there might be trouble, Tucker tensed, ready to move if necessary, but the woman deftly extricated herself and shook her head.

"Keep your hat on, Trent," she told him, sidestepping another pass. "I'll bring a round of beer for everyone in a minute."

Glancing at Garrett, Tucker noticed he, too, appeared to be concerned. When she disappeared behind the bar, he turned to Tucker. "Good to see you've joined us."

"Yeah, it's my first time," Tucker admitted. "As an adult, that is." He pointed to the coffee in front of Garrett. "You must stop in often if the waitress knows your order."

Garrett laughed. "Libby's good. She hasn't been in town long, but she learned fast what the customers want."

"The sign of a good waitress."

Garrett nodded and took a sip of his coffee. Morgan said something to him, and Tucker turned his attention to his brother, who was deep in conversation with Dusty about their stock company. Leaning back, Tucker listened, while he watched the things going on around him. For some people, being an observer might have been awkward, but for him, it was the way he'd spent the biggest part of his life. As a teenager on the rodeo circuit, he hadn't wanted to be found and tried not to answer questions about his personal life, so he'd remained quiet and did a lot of listening.

He'd learned a lot, too. That's where he'd first heard about the Marine Corps. Once he was in the service, he continued to keep his personal life to himself, but he got to know his fellow marines. Sometimes he thought he knew some of them better than they knew themselves. Yet they knew very little about him, and that's the way he'd liked it. Staying in the background suited him just fine. He still had no desire to be the center of attention.

The waitress returned with the sandwiches and set them on the table. "Is there anything else I can get you gentlemen?"

"Tucker?" Garrett asked. "A beer, maybe?"

"Sure, that'd be fine." Now that he was no longer taking the pain medication, he didn't see a reason why he couldn't imbibe a little. But a little was all he'd drink. His real drinking days had not only peaked, but also ended when he was young. Oh, he'd had a few wild nights after he'd joined the Corps, but they'd become fewer and farther between. He chalked it up to being older and wiser.

"How about you, Garrett?" the waitress asked.

He shook his head. "No, I'm fine with the coffee. Have you met Tucker O'Brien?"

She turned to Tucker with a smile. "No, I haven't. You must be Tanner's brother." She wiped her hand on the short apron she wore and held it out to him. "I'm Libby. Libby Carter."

"Nice to meet you, Libby," Tucker said, taking her hand for a moment. There was no rush when he touched her like there was when he touched Paige. He knew that wasn't a good sign. He had no business getting involved with anyone, but he'd been too attracted to Paige and had let it go too far. She made him feel things he didn't remember ever feeling, and feelings weren't something he dealt with very well. He never should have made love to her, but it was too late now. And, no matter what, he didn't regret it.

"How 'bout those beers, Libby?" the cowboy in the blue shirt asked again.

Libby turned to look at him, but before she could say anything, another player answered. "Give it a rest, Trent. You've still got half a bottle on the table."

"Maybe I want a cold one." Trent called to Libby as she walked away, then he moved around the table, to stand in front of the other player. "If she'd stop flirtin' with the *city attorney,* there, maybe we'd get some service."

No one gave any notice to the sound of a cell phone ringing. Tucker saw Garrett give a small, imperceptible shake of his head when he answered it. Trent was now directly behind him, and Tucker decided things were heating up too fast for comfort. Libby had thankfully disappeared.

"Let's get back to the game," the other player said.

"So take your shot," Trent grumbled, but didn't seem to notice when Garrett left the table and walked away, the phone to his ear. "I don't care what you do. But I want my beer."

The other player leaned over the pool table, ready to take his shot, and answered calmly. "And I want to finish this game. Maybe if you hadn't had a bottle in your hand all night, you might've beat me, but you're way behind now."

Tucker watched as Trent grabbed his beer bottle from a nearby table and took a swig from it. Moving closer to the other player, enough to bump against the end of his stick, he laughed. "You think I'm drunk? You ain't seen nothin'."

"Don't want to, either. Now back up and let me take this shot, then we'll call this game a draw."

There was a blur of motion, and Tucker was on his feet. Trent's beer bottle fell to the floor with a crash of glass, as Tucker knocked it out of his hand when Trent went to bring it down on the other player's head. Tucker had Trent's arm angled behind his back and was moving him toward the exit.

"I'd stay real quiet, if I were you," Tucker whispered in his ear as he shoved the tavern door open with Trent's body. Slamming the man up against the side of the building, he shoved Trent's arm up higher, until Trent finally cried out. It was then that Tucker realized where he was and what he was doing, and eased his grip.

Turning at the sound of the door opening, Tucker saw Morgan walk out of the tavern.

"Good work," Morgan told him, taking the arm Tucker held and putting on the handcuffs. "My deputy's on his way. Trent doesn't usually get so mean." Turning Trent around to face him, he sighed. "I gave you a warning a couple of months ago, but this time you've stepped over the line. A night in a cell will give you time to sober up and think."

Tucker realized he was no longer needed and turned for the tavern, but Morgan called to him. "Don't leave. I'd like to talk to you, if you have some time."

Tucker wondered if he'd have been better off minding his own business. He hadn't meant to grab the guy or cause any trouble, but when he'd seen Trent raise that beer bottle, ready to use it as a weapon, he knew the other player was in for some hurt, and he reacted without thinking. He could imagine how upset Morgan might be. After all, Tucker knew he didn't have any right to do what he'd done.

Inside, the tavern noise had quieted some, and the pool game had apparently ended when Tucker had escorted Trent outside. Tucker was thankful everyone was choosing to go about their business, and no one at the table other than Tanner mentioned what had taken place.

"Everything okay?" Tanner asked, when Tucker returned to their table.

"Yeah," Tucker answered, but he wasn't sure what Morgan would have to say to him. He'd really stepped out of line, this time, he was sure.

Less than ten minutes later, Morgan was giving him a friendly slap on the back. "Grab your beer and come over here."

Tucker nodded, grabbed his bottle and followed Morgan to a small table away from the others. "Look, I know I was out of line—"

"It's a good thing you were," Morgan said quickly. "I should've been quicker, but I know Trent, and I didn't expect anything like that from him. I'm just glad you were so quick and diffused the situation before somebody was hurt."

"I just— It happened before I realized what I was doing," Tucker admitted.

Nodding, Morgan smiled. "Like I said, it's a good thing. Thanks for reacting so quickly."

Embarrassed, Tucker only nodded.

"You know," Morgan began, leaning back in his chair, "I could use another deputy. There's only two of us, and I've finally managed to get the city council's approval to hire another. You'd sure be an asset for us."

Surprised, Tucker wasn't sure what to think, much less say.

"I can't imagine doing anything like that," he said, honestly. "And I doubt that I could pass a physical. There's a rod in my lower leg, and I've had ACL surgery on my knee."

Morgan nodded. "I can understand your hesitancy, especially with the injuries, but we'd take that into account." He leaned forward. "You know what a small town this is," he said. "You grew up here. Most of the time it's quiet, with nothing more than an occasional dust-up like tonight." He leaned back again and ran his hand down his face. "I'll admit that there was a problem a year or so ago, and even I came to understand that anyplace could be dangerous, under the right circumstances. But that's rare, I can assure you. You have the training to deal with those things. Just look at how you handled Trent."

Tucker did think about it, and he thought about how he'd nearly lost his temper with the man, before Morgan had stepped outside. Sure, he had the training, but he also had experiences that few people had, and those experiences made him different than others.

Those experiences also made it impossible for him to ever get close to anyone, even if he'd wanted to. Paige had managed to make him start feeling again, but he didn't want that. He liked the numbness he'd felt for so long.

"I appreciate your offer," he finally told Morgan, "but I can't take the job. Not right now."

Not ever.

Chapter Ten

"Any pain?" Paige asked Tucker as she moved his leg, testing the flexibility of his knee.

"Not a bit, even when Nikki and I went riding on Tuesday."

Alarm that he'd risked reinjuring his leg caused Paige to look up at him. "I thought we discussed that," she said.

What might have been a smile was now a frown. "We were careful, I promise."

More careful than they'd been about using protection? she wanted to ask, as she ducked her head and continued to flex his knee. But she'd already admitted to herself that it was as much her fault as his, maybe even more. After all, she was a doctor and knew the risks. Not just about pregnancy—and thankfully there was very little chance anything like that had occurred, considering the timing. She didn't even want to think about what could have happened had that timing been different. No, there were other repercussions, such as STDs and HIV. But even that wasn't what bothered her. She knew he was clean. She'd seen his medical files.

"Paige?"

Unwilling at the moment to look at him, she released

his leg and stepped back. "Everything checks out great," she told him as she moved to put away the instruments. "In fact, it's so great that I don't see any reason for you to come in again."

"Yeah?" There was a note of relief in his voice. "So I'm released?"

"Unofficially," she answered, "because none of this was official to begin with."

"And I haven't thanked you for that," he said. "In fact, I was downright mean at times."

She smiled, remembering just how difficult it had been in the beginning, but she didn't turn around to face him. "Don't worry about it. The important thing is that you can walk without a cane, and especially without pain."

"Yeah, it is," he agreed. "So what do you say about a little celebration?"

Taken off balance, she turned to stare at him. "Celebration?"

"Sure. I owe you, and I was thinking maybe I could take you out to dinner or something. Tonight, maybe?"

Dinner with Tucker was out of the question, and she shook her head. "You don't owe me anything." She turned back to the cupboard and began straightening it. Anything to keep herself busy.

"Then think of another reason."

She felt him close behind her, but refused to turn around. "It isn't necessary," she repeated.

"Why not?" he asked. "You took time out of your life to help me. You didn't have to. As you pointed out, you're a doctor, not a physical therapist. Yet you agreed to help."

"Somebody had to," she answered, and then turned around. He was standing so close, it wouldn't have taken anything to reach out and touch him. She didn't. That, she knew, would've been wrong.

He was quiet for a moment as he watched her. "It's because of what happened last Saturday, isn't it?"

Her breath caught. "No." She instantly regretted the lie, but she couldn't change it.

"That kind of thing is against the rules, isn't it?"

Silently, she nodded.

"No hanky-panky between the doctor and the patient," he continued. "Even when you were being a friend, not a doctor. And you're all about the rules, aren't you?"

Nodding, she sighed, as threatening tears burned her eyes. "I have to be. I worked hard to become a doctor. I could lose my license over it."

He moved closer and brushed her cheek with his hand. "Nobody is going to know about it, unless one of us tells someone. That won't be me."

Unable to speak and fearing tears would start falling if she even tried, she nodded.

"So let's go celebrate the end of my therapy with some dinner." When she started to shake her head again, he put a finger under her chin and lifted her head, his eyes meeting hers. "A simple dinner, nothing fancy, *not* in Desperation." He hesitated and smiled. "And I promise to behave. So what do you say?"

She didn't want to say no, but she wasn't sure she could say yes. Warring with herself, she convinced herself that he'd never technically been her therapy patient, there wasn't a reason she couldn't say yes. "All right," she answered, unable to hide her smile. "Let me lock up, and I'll meet you out back."

For a brief moment, she thought he was going to kiss her, but he stepped back instead. "Don't be long," he said, walking to the door to the hallway. "Friday nights are always busy."

Five minutes later, she stepped out the back door and made sure it was locked. When she turned around, Tucker jumped out of his SUV and hurried to open the passenger door for her. Settled inside, they were on their way in minutes.

As they headed out of town, she asked, "Where's this place we're going?"

"North of Edmond."

"That far?" she asked.

He turned to smile at her. "Yeah, but the food is worth it."

"I'll take your word for it," she said, and settled in for a longer ride than she'd expected.

They talked about the high school baseball team, then they talked about everything—except what had happened between them and how they felt about it.

They'd been driving along for several minutes, each wrapped in their own thoughts, when Tucker cleared his throat. "I've been wanting to ask you something."

Unsure of what he might be referring to and a little nervous about it, she cautiously asked, "What's that?"

"Do you know what I like best about you?"

If they hadn't been traveling at sixty plus miles an hour, she might have been tempted to grab the door handle. Instead, she simply replied, "No. What?"

"You didn't give up on me."

Paige wasn't sure how to answer. "I guess it takes a

stubborn person to deal with another stubborn person," she answered.

"It was more than that." He took his eyes off the road ahead long enough for her to see he was serious. "You just kept insisting that I do some physical therapy, no matter what I said. Why?"

She'd never shared the experience with Jeff with anyone, not even her dad, who was a surgeon and would have understood. Glancing at Tucker in the seat beside her, she realized it might be time to tell the story. Once shared, it might no longer hold the power it had.

"I was doing a rotation when I was an intern, learning all kinds of aspects of medicine," she began slowly. "One of the patients we visited was a young man who'd received a spinal injury from a dive that had left him paralyzed and in a wheelchair."

"How old was he?"

"Early twenties," she answered as a vivid memory of Jeff, looking up at her with his beautiful smile, drifted into her mind. "I used to stop in and see him before I left the hospital for the day, no matter how tired I was."

"That doesn't surprise me," he said softly.

She smiled, but didn't respond to the remark. "Two years earlier, he and some friends had been out partying on the nearby river, where there was an old, unused railroad bridge. There was drinking and dares were made, not for the first time, to dive off the bridge. They'd taken the dive before, and all had been well."

"Riverbeds shift," Tucker said, in the dark confines of his vehicle.

"That's the one thing they didn't think about," Paige whispered. "From what I heard, Jeff had originally taken it in stride, but as time went on and by the time I met him, he'd fallen into a deep depression. He'd stopped the therapy that he needed and was back in the hospital. He told me once that he didn't have anything to live for." She stopped and took a deep breath. "I guess he didn't think he did."

They were silent for a moment, before Tucker spoke. "What happened to him?"

Paige couldn't stop her sigh. "Officially it was an accidental overdose of the medications he was taking. I think it was much more than that."

"I guess I can understand why you were so tough with me." He slowed the SUV and pulled into a parking lot north of Edmond, found an empty space and turned off the engine.

She turned toward him, hoping he would understand. "It wasn't the lack of physical therapy that killed him, although in time, considering his injury, it could have," she whispered. "It was his despondency that killed him. He truly believed there was nothing left to live for, and I think he took an overdose on purpose. He was wrong. Except for being confined to that wheelchair, he was a vibrant, funny, intelligent young man."

Reaching out, Tucker took her hand. "I'm sorry, Paige."

"It was a long time ago, but you asked why I kept at you. I hope you understand."

"I do."

"Good." She didn't regret having told him, but she was glad it was over. "Can we eat now?"

TUCKER COULDN'T REMEMBER having a more enjoyable evening. He'd chosen the restaurant for several reasons. First, it was far from Desperation and the atmosphere was casual. And second, the place was co-owned by a marine he'd served with when he'd first joined the Corps, long before he'd become special ops. When Rick saw them come in, he stopped at the table to say hello, and Tucker introduced him to Paige, before business called Rick away.

The food was as good as promised and they took their time eating. Conversation was easy both at the restaurant and on the way home, much later that night. Paige talked about growing up in a medical family in Chicago. Not only was her father a doctor, but her mother was also a retired surgical nurse. She joked about her brother being the family disappointment by going into law, instead of medicine, but it was plain to see that she was as proud of him as she said her parents were.

Tucker shared memories of growing up on the ranch, going to rodeos to see his mother ride and how he'd dreamed of being a rodeo star when he grew up. Keeping stories of his experiences in the Corps to a minimum, he shared happier tales of travel and seeing the world. By the time they were on their way home, he was wishing the evening didn't have to end, but he knew that wasn't possible for him. It would all end soon. There was no reason to think it wouldn't.

At the clinic parking lot, he walked her to her car, thanked her for a wonderful evening and managed not to take her in his arms. After he'd followed her home to make sure she arrived safely, he drove slowly down the empty streets of Desperation, wishing again that his life had been much different, but knowing he'd had opportunities he'd refused to take.

He hadn't meant to disturb Tanner, but his brother

looked up when Tucker walked past the open door of the ranch office. "You're in late," Tanner said.

Tucker didn't see any reason not to be honest and he stopped. "I took Paige up to a place north of Edmond for dinner. One of the owners is an old friend from the Corps."

"By the look of you, I'd say you enjoyed yourself."

Tucker didn't want to say too much and give Tanner the wrong idea, so he answered with, "She's a nice lady."

"We sure think so. Desperation was lucky to get her."

"Yeah," Tucker answered. "Well, I guess I'll turn in."

He'd taken two steps when he heard Tanner clear his throat. "If you have a few minutes…"

Stopping, Tucker turned back. "Sure."

As Tucker stepped into the room, Tanner moved from behind the big, solid wood desk that had been their father's, and leaned against the front edge of it. "I owe you an apology," Tanner said, as Tucker took one of the upholstered chairs that sat facing it, just as he had when he was a boy.

Tucker rubbed his palms on the arms of the chair, wondering what had gotten into his older brother. "For what?" he asked.

"You were right about letting Shawn go to that graduation party," Tanner said. "He's eighteen. He's proven that he's a responsible adult. He's going to drive halfway across the country with Ryan in less than a week. It's time to let him make his own decisions."

Tucker nodded. "And maybe I should've kept my mouth shut."

"Why would you think that?" Tanner asked. "He's your son."

"And I wasn't around to raise him." Just saying it made his heart heavy. "You didn't have much of a choice, did you?"

Tanner chuckled, but it held little humor. "I have to admit that when a girl I'd never seen before came to the door with a six-month-old baby in her arms and told me you were the father, I was pretty much speechless."

"You were engaged to… What was her name?"

"She didn't take too kindly to me having a baby," Tanner answered, without mentioning the name. "It probably saved me from making a major mistake I would've regretted forever, so Shawn was a blessing in disguise."

"But you had a clue how to be a father," Tucker reminded him. "After trying to tame me, that is."

Tanner glanced at the floor. When he looked up, his mouth was set in a grim line. "I never wanted the job of being your father, Tucker. It was more responsibility than I knew how to handle, and I made a mess of it."

"I guess we both did," Tucker admitted.

"I was too hard on you," Tanner continued. "I didn't know what to do. I didn't know how to keep you in line. You always had that wild streak. That…" He shrugged.

"Wanderlust," Tucker said. "That's what Dad said about Mom. Even Grandmother Ayita used that word."

Tanner nodded. "Yeah, that would be it, I guess. You took after Sally. I was afraid Shawn was going to do the same thing when he was fourteen or fifteen. If it hadn't been for Jules, I'm not sure he'd still be here. I wasn't handling it much better than I did with you. I know it was my fault you left and—"

"No," Tucker said. "At least no more your fault than mine. I was pretty headstrong, determined to ride the circuit and be a big rodeo star." He laughed and shook his head. "Pretty ironic that you're the one who won the championship. I didn't have it in me, so I'm damn proud to tell people you're my brother."

"No more proud than I am of you for getting the help you needed for your knee and leg."

Tucker had suspected the family had guessed he was working with Paige. "I did it for Shawn," he told Tanner. "At first, anyway. Then when I started actually seeing improvement—and especially when I could walk up the stairs without a twinge—there wasn't any way I was going to give up for anything."

"So you're finished? Paige isn't working with you on the therapy?"

"We're finished." Tucker realized that he meant that in more ways than one. He and Tanner had come full circle and somehow worked out the problems from their past—at least as much as possible. It was time to move on.

As Tucker moved to stand, Tanner stopped him. "Before you go…"

"What?"

Tanner didn't directly look at him. "You aren't the only one in this family with relationship problems. Before Jules, I really believed that if I loved somebody, they'd leave. Imagine what I went through when Jules came along."

"I didn't know," Tucker answered. "She was able to help you, though."

"Eventually I came to my senses, but while she was dealing with her own problems. She didn't like my career and left me over it."

Tucker looked at him. "Really?"

Nodding, Tanner smiled. "Someday we'll tell you about it. Tucker, nobody is perfect, and the O'Briens seem to have more than their share of problems. We manage to do some things that are right, though."

Still surprised at his brother's revelation, Tucker got to his feet and held out his hand. Tanner pushed away from the edge of the desk and took it in his, giving it a squeeze. "Let's put the past behind us and be the brothers we should've been," he suggested.

Tucker, feeling his throat tighten, nodded. Before he could manage to say anything, the phone on the desk rang and Tanner reached for it. "See you at breakfast?"

"I'll be there," Tucker replied. He didn't add that it would probably be the last meal he'd share with his family, at least for a long time. Now that he and Tanner had made their peace...now that he'd gotten to know his son, but would never know those years he missed, it was time to move on.

As he climbed the stairs to his room, he thought about the past. So much had happened since that early morning almost twenty years ago when he'd stolen away before the sun came up and walked to the county road, where he found a ride headed anywhere.

If anyone had told him on that crisp fall morning that he'd return to the Rocking O someday, he would have laughed. If they'd told him the same thing three years later, as he signed the recruitment papers, he'd have laughed even harder. Yet here he was, and he was glad he'd come. But it was time to move on. He'd tell Shawn tomorrow that he wouldn't be there for graduation and hoped his son understood. It was Tanner who had raised the boy Tucker hadn't known about, and it was Tanner who deserved to experience this last rite of passage with the boy who was like his son.

"HEY, DAD."

Tucker shoved the box farther inside his SUV and turned, shading his eyes against the morning sun with his hand. Shawn stood in the yard, a dark silhouette. Tucker had hoped he could get everything packed before anyone noticed. Apparently things weren't going to go as he'd hoped.

"Are you coming in for breakfast?" Shawn asked, walking closer.

Tucker pulled the hatchback down until it clicked. "Sure."

"What are you doing with those boxes?" Shawn asked, nodding toward the back of the SUV.

"Just some stuff." Tucker put his arm around Shawn's shoulders and turned toward the house, trying to avoid the inevitable, at least for a while. "Have you and Ryan decided when you're leaving for the coast?"

"Maybe on Thursday," Shawn answered, as they stepped up on the wide porch together and started around for the back to the kitchen. "We want to get an early start, and that probably won't work on Wednesday. You know, with that party and all, Tuesday night after the graduation ceremony."

Tucker felt more than saw the glance Shawn gave him. "Smart thinking. No sense taking risks that don't need to be taken."

Shawn opened the back door and held it for Tucker, then followed him inside the house. "That's pretty much what Ryan and I thought. One day isn't going to make that much difference. We aren't in a rush, or anything, to get there."

"There you are," Bridey called to them. "Tucker, there's scrambled eggs and ham. And don't miss the doughnuts Kate dropped off early this morning."

"I wondered who was stopping by so early," he said, taking a seat at the table with the rest of the family. "She must be a morning person to be up and about that early."

Jules handed him a cup of coffee. "She worked Aggie's farm for years, and you know how it is for farmers."

"Up at dawn, in bed at dusk," he said.

"Well, not so much at dusk," Jules said, laughing. "I know I'd never be able to get to sleep that early."

Bridey handed him a plate of fresh-baked biscuits, and he breathed in the smell of them. "I sure missed your cooking all those years," he told his aunt.

She stopped, quiet for a moment, then a smile brightened her face. "We missed *you,* Tucker. And you'll never have to miss my cooking again."

He tried to smile back at her, but instead, he ducked his head. Staring at the plate full of food in front of him, he felt a wave of shame pass over him. He'd done his family wrong in the past. There was no doubt they'd worried about him. Tanner had admitted to hiring private detectives to try to find him, and he could imagine how Bridey had reacted. He knew he'd been her favorite when he was a young boy. But she hadn't been able to take the place of the mother who'd left him.

He'd wondered for a while if it had been his fault that Sally had left. Bridey had always been there when he'd needed comforting and had assured him it didn't have anything to do with him, his brother or his daddy. His mama just wasn't a person who could stay in one place. But it was years before he could accept that he wasn't at fault, at least in some small way.

It wasn't easy to keep up with the everyday conversation when his mind was on how he was going to explain to Shawn why he wasn't sticking around. Nobody seemed concerned when he didn't say much. Maybe it was because he'd been there long enough that everyone understood he wasn't much for talking.

As soon as breakfast was over, he went up to his room to pack the last of his belongings. He hadn't had much to begin with. He'd been living light for most of his life. When he wasn't living in a barracks, he'd lived in a small apartment. Living alone was his choice, although he'd had a couple of roommates over the years. He liked solitude better.

With an oversize and overstuffed duffel bag in each hand, he surveyed the room for anything he might have missed. Tanner had given him photos of Shawn over the years, but those were carefully tucked away in a solid box with a few other bits of memorabilia.

He was ready.

No one was around when he reached the bottom of the stairs and turned for the front door. Even on a Saturday, there were chores to keep everyone busy, at least for part of the morning.

At his SUV, he stowed the duffels in the back. His intention was to find Shawn and let him know he was moving on, but he didn't need to look for him. As soon as he shut the rear door and turned around, Shawn was walking toward him from the barn.

"You're leaving," Shawn said, stopping in front of Tucker.

"It's time I move on."

Shawn's mouth turned down in a frown, and he planted his hands on his hips. "Why? Did I do something wrong?"

"Of course not," Tucker replied.

"I thought you were staying for my graduation."

Tucker nodded and tried to keep any hint of the emotions that were rolling inside of him from showing. "I'd planned to, but I think that's something that you and your uncle should share, without me around."

"That's crazy." For a moment Shawn said nothing else, then his eyes narrowed. "Did he tell you to leave? Is that it? Is it about that party?"

"This is my decision, and Tanner doesn't know. Don't blame him, Shawn. He did a good job raising you. He loves you."

"And I love him, too," Shawn said, his eyes shimmering with tears. "But you're my dad, even though I never knew you until a few weeks ago. You don't know what it's been like."

"I have an idea," Tucker said, before Shawn could say more. "It's plain that you're a better person than I am. I didn't stay, and then I was irresponsible enough to father a child and not even know. You've been much better off having Tanner around."

Shawn shook his head, whipping it from side to side. "You don't understand! Getting to know you is the best thing that's ever happened to me."

Tucker's throat closed on the emotions welling inside,

but he remained determined to do what he believed was right. "You're grown up now, Shawn. You don't need me. You're an adult, getting ready to strike out on your own."

Shawn looked around the yard, as if he was looking for something. "I'll be back in a couple of months," he said, a note of panic in his voice. "I might be going to college, but I'll be coming home on weekends and holidays. I'd thought you'd be here then. I'd *expected* you to be here."

"I know." Tucker didn't want to be a disappointment, but he knew what was best. Maybe Shawn didn't realize that the ties would soon be broken, no matter what, but Tucker understood how quickly life changed when a young man struck out on his own. "We'll keep in touch, I promise. What with all the fancy technology, we can talk anytime."

Shawn shook his head slowly. "It isn't the same." Looking up, he looked steadily at Tucker. "If you won't do it for me, maybe you'll do it for her."

"Her?" Tucker said, without thinking. But then he knew who Shawn meant, and he didn't have an answer.

Obviously resigned by the slump of his shoulders, Shawn sighed. "Where are you headed?"

Knowing he needed to leave now, before he couldn't, Tucker moved around to the driver's side of the vehicle. "I haven't decided."

"You have my cell phone number?" Shawn asked.

Tucker nodded.

"Then let me know when you do decide."

"I will." Standing at the door, he reached out and

pulled his son into his arms, giving him a hug. "Have Tanner send me pictures of graduation, okay?"

"Okay." But Shawn's voice was muffled and shaky.

"And have a safe trip to the coast."

Shawn nodded, his chin bumping against Tucker's chest. "We will."

Tucker finally released him and opened the door to climb in.

"I'm glad I finally met you," Shawn said. "I just wish you'd stay."

"I'm glad I finally met you, too," Tucker replied.

He could still see Shawn standing in the drive before he turned onto the dirt road that would lead him away from the Rocking O, yet again. But there was one more stop he needed to make before he hit the road.

Chapter Eleven

Paige nudged the front door open with her shoulder and prayed she wouldn't drop the armload of files she was carrying. She'd already decided she wouldn't bother to open them until tomorrow. She and Garrett were going to the O'Briens' tonight for a pregraduation barbecue, and she was ready to kick back and relax. Or at least try to.

"You're home early," Garrett greeted her when she stepped inside.

She shut the door and smiled at him. "We even stayed an extra half hour after the last scheduled patient, but nobody else came in. I'm free for the rest of the day."

"Obviously not too free," Garrett said, nodding at the files still in her arms.

"I'll deal with them tomorrow," she said with a shrug. "Right now, I'm going to change, and then I'm going to relax on the deck for a few minutes and enjoy this lovely spring afternoon. Then I'll check on those flowers I planted. I'm sure they need some water, if not a little weeding."

In her bedroom, she dropped the files and her purse on the bureau, and then changed into a pair of shorts and a T-shirt from her college days. After slipping on a pair of canvas shoes, she grabbed her sunglasses and walked through the house and out onto the deck.

With a sigh of contentment, she lowered herself into the cushioned lounger and closed her eyes. Spring was definitely in the air. Thanks to a light breeze, the scent of newly opened flowers drifted her way. It was times like this that reminded her of how right her move to Desperation had been. She'd been resistant to Garrett's suggestion to move from the beginning, but when the group of doctors she shared her practice with in Cincinnati decided on a new set of rules…she was more than ready for a move. Since the very first day she arrived in Desperation, she'd never regretted the change, and she often thanked Garrett for continuing to insist. And for allowing her to live in his house. One day, soon, she'd find a place of her own, but neither of them was in a hurry to make changes. With both of them working late hours, they rarely saw each other. Meals were whatever they could get, except on Sundays, when she tried to make a nice dinner for the two of them. But too often, Garrett was out of town, and their family time, as they called it, didn't happen.

She wouldn't have believed it if someone had told her that she'd love small-town living, but now she wouldn't trade it for anything.

"Somebody's here to see you, Paige."

She turned around at the sound of her brother's voice and saw Tucker stepping out onto the deck. "I hope this isn't a bad time," he said. "I stopped at the clinic, but everyone was gone."

Her heart raced and she hoped he didn't notice how nervous she was. Why was he here? They'd agreed his therapy was over. "We finished the day early," she explained, trying to appear calm and unaffected, then waved at a nearby chair. "Sit down, won't you?"

"Thanks." Sitting, he looked around. "It's nice out here."

"The flowers need watering and weeding, and Garrett's not into digging in the dirt." She shrugged. "I came out to take care of it and decided to enjoy what's left of the afternoon."

He nodded and didn't look directly at her. "Do you like to garden?"

She laughed, thinking of how limited her time was. "When I can. Which isn't often, but I try."

When he nodded again, but was silent, she began to feel a little uneasy. Looking at him more closely, she wondered if something was bothering him. *He* looked a little nervous.

"Was there something specific you wanted to talk about?" she asked, needing to know what was going on and if something was wrong.

"There is," he answered, but he didn't seem to be any more at ease than she was feeling.

"Is your knee bothering you?" she asked, suddenly more concerned. "Or your leg?"

"No, no," he said quickly. "Everything is good with that, which is why I'm here, I guess."

A feeling of dread snaked up her back. "Oh?" And he still didn't look directly at her.

This time, he nodded. "Yeah. I wanted to thank you for everything you did for me."

"You already did that," she reminded him.

"Yes and no. I told you that if it hadn't been for you, I never would have done the physical therapy." He shifted in the chair and finally looked at her, their gazes locking. "You saved me, Paige. You're my miracle worker."

A hard knot formed in the pit of her stomach. Something was going on. She could sense it, but she didn't know what it was. "I only made you do what you needed to do. *You* did the work, not me. And you were the one who came to me, ready to do it."

"But if you hadn't kept at me—"

Paige was on her feet. "I'm not a miracle worker. I'm a doctor. It's my job to help people." She spun around and pointed at him. "Especially people like you, too stubborn to do what's good for them. I don't know what this is about, but—" Suddenly, seeing his eyes watching her, she knew. "You're leaving." When he didn't answer, she continued. "When? *Now?*"

He nodded, and she couldn't believe this was happening. Her heart ached. Tears threatened, but she wouldn't let him see. "But Shawn's graduation is Tuesday. Aren't you going to at least wait for that? I know you were planning to be there. It's the reason you stayed and—"

"My plans changed," he said simply.

She opened her mouth to reply, but there was nothing she could say. She knew that. What she felt didn't matter. She'd been denying that she'd fallen in love with him, but she had. She'd risked her career in the weight room, and she hadn't cared. For some strange reason, she thought something might come of it, even though she kept telling herself it couldn't.

"Does Shawn know?" she finally managed to ask.

"I told him before I came here," he said, getting up from the chair and taking a step toward her. "I didn't want to leave without seeing you first."

She moved away from him. "Are you saying he's all right with this?"

"He understands."

She shook her head and turned away. "I—I can't believe this."

He took her arm. "Paige, I—"

She turned back to look at him, but all she saw in his eyes was pain. And she didn't understand. He was the one who'd decided to leave, for whatever crazy reason.

"I'm damaged goods, Paige. You don't have any idea. My life— Well, it hasn't been what most people would call normal. I've never been able to settle down, not even in the marines. I'm a loner, and I'll always be a loner. You'd only— I don't want to hurt you."

She didn't believe him, except that he didn't want to share his life with anyone, and especially with her. Shame swept through her that she had actually allowed a thought, here and there, of the two of them having some kind of future. But she still wasn't ready to give up. "Maybe I'm willing to take that chance."

Looking away, he shook his head. "You don't understand."

"Then explain it to me," she begged, not caring how it might appear. "Help me understand."

He started to speak, but instead, he released her. "There's no way I can thank you—"

"Then don't." Speaking was difficult as she fought the tears that clogged her throat. "I don't need your thanks."

"Paige—"

"What I need..." she began and then realized this wasn't about her. "No, what you need is to forgive yourself for all those things you think you did wrong, all those bad choices. When you can let go of all that misplaced guilt that's weighing down your heart, then you can move forward, instead of being mired in a past that you can't seem to realize is over and done with. Only then will you be a whole person."

He shook his head. "You don't—"

"Understand?" she finished, knowing that was what he was going to say. "Yes, I do, so don't waste your time telling me, because it won't make a difference. Not to me, and definitely not to you. Goodbye, Tucker. Have a happy life."

He stood watching her for a few moments, then turned and walked into the house.

When she heard the sound of his vehicle starting, and then driving away, she gave up holding back the tears. Reaching for a trowel, she ordered herself not to think about what had just happened. It was for the best. She didn't need him, and he certainly didn't need her. Not anymore.

PAIGE STEPPED INTO the house and closed the sliding glass patio door behind her. Glancing at her watch, she realized she'd stayed outside longer than she'd realized. At least the garden was weeded and her flowers were watered. Other than that, she didn't care to think.

"There you are," Garrett said when she walked into the living room. "Jules O'Brien called and asked if we could come a little early. I told her I didn't think it would be a problem."

Stopping, Paige took a deep breath. She wanted to tell her brother to call Jules back and tell her they wouldn't be coming. Or at least *she* wouldn't be. Garrett could go if he wanted to. But she knew if she did that it would raise questions she couldn't answer. Not now. Maybe not ever.

"It isn't a problem," Paige answered, but her heart just wasn't in it. It would be obvious to everyone that Tucker was gone, which would probably be the topic of discussion. Could she handle it?

Garrett stepped closer, gently taking her arm and turning her to face him. "Is everything okay?"

"Of course it is." She attempted to slip away, but he held on to her, watching her closely. "All right, it isn't," she admitted, but she couldn't be completely honest with him. "It has nothing to do with me, but it affects all of the O'Briens. I think that's why Jules asked if we could come early."

Apparently he still wasn't willing to release her. "Do you want to let me in on what's going on? I hate to be the only one there in the dark."

She didn't see any reason not to tell him. "Tucker has left the ranch."

"Is he coming back?"

Shaking her head, she hoped she could keep her voice level. "No, it doesn't appear he is."

Garrett's nod was slow and then there was understanding in his eyes. "Then we'll do whatever you think is best. If you want to stay home—"

"No," she said, almost too quickly. "We'll go."

Garrett didn't ask questions later as he drove them out to the Rocking O, but Paige knew he had them. They'd been in high school when the big blowup about getting into the other's business happened. It was then that they'd made a pact that if they suspected something was wrong with the other, there'd be no questions or discussion until they both agreed. It still worked well for them. For the time being, Paige wasn't agreeable to talking about what had happened with Tucker. For one thing, she didn't completely understand it, and for another, she was embarrassed that she'd let herself get carried away and endangered her career.

Jules answered the door when they rang the bell. "I'm glad you could both make it," she greeted them both. "Garrett, Tanner is out on the patio. I think a couple of the boys from the Bent Tree are with him, and Wyoming, too, so go on out. Nikki and Mac will be there soon." As soon as Garrett was out of earshot, Jules turned to Paige. "Thanks for coming early. I guess you know Tucker has gone?"

Paige nodded.

"I didn't want to talk about this in front of everyone and calling off the evening wouldn't change anything," Jules said with a sigh. "Tanner is more upset than I ever remember seeing him. He thought they'd worked out all their problems yesterday."

"Is there anything I can do to help?" Paige knew it was weak, but it's all she had. She felt as blindsided as Jules obviously did.

"Let's talk in Tanner's office," Jules said, keeping her voice low, and she led Paige around the corner and down a short hallway.

"Wow," Paige said, when they stepped into the room. "This is definitely a man's room."

Jules laughed as she indicated a sofa along one wall. "Not a thing has been changed in it except to add a computer since it was Tanner's father's." When they were both seated on the sofa, she turned to Paige. "Have you talked to Tucker in the past two days?"

"He came by this afternoon."

"Do you know where he's going?"

Paige could only shake her head. She knew so little. She understood even less.

Jules reached out and squeezed her hand. "I thought things were better and he was going to stay."

"What about Shawn?"

Sighing, Jules leaned her head back against the sofa. "Apparently Shawn was the first to know his dad was leaving. He asked Tucker if he was going to be back for graduation, but Tucker said he wouldn't be. Something about Tanner being the one who raised him. I don't know." She turned her head to look at Paige. "He's all right physically, isn't he?"

"He's fine," Paige assured her, feeling a little better within her own area of knowledge. "But it's not his body, it's his mind. His heart. He doesn't seem to be able to forgive himself for the choices he made."

"And so he makes even more bad ones," Jules said, shaking her head. "I tried to get him to go for some counseling, but he said he didn't need it." She looked directly at Paige before continuing. "I was hoping you might have some sway with him about that sort of thing. While you were working with him on his therapy, that is."

Paige knew exactly what Jules wasn't saying, and she decided maybe they should get some things out in the open, so nothing was misunderstood. "I helped him with his therapy," she admitted, "but he did the work on his own. All I did was give him instructions and monitor his progress, nothing more."

"He seemed to be hiding it from everyone."

"I don't think he wanted anyone making a big deal

of it," Paige explained. "And, too, I think that in the beginning he was afraid he would fail, so he kept it secret."

"He does care about his family," Jules said, her voice almost a whisper. "More than himself, I think."

"No one can say he has a big ego," Paige agreed. "He'd rather walk away than hurt people, but he doesn't realize how walking away hurts everyone. Even him."

With a sigh, Jules got to her feet. "You and I have been in similar situations. I have everything needed to help him emotionally, yet I'm his sister-in-law and too close to work with him, while you couldn't treat him because your heart was involved."

Paige jumped up. "Jules—"

"It's all right, Paige," Jules said, pressing a hand to her shoulder. "I completely understand. When I first met Tanner, he believed that the people he loved always left him. He even feared Shawn was going to leave. I had the ability and the training to help, but I couldn't help Tanner for the same reason you couldn't, and it took some time for him to realize how wrong he was."

"At least he did," Paige said, as they left the room. "I'm not sure the same will be said for Tucker."

"Don't give up yet. He won't be gone forever. I'm sure of it."

Paige didn't feel at all cheered. "I'm not counting on anything, when it comes to Tucker."

Before Jules could answer, the doorbell rang. Jules went to the door, while Paige made her way slowly to the patio at the back of the house, thinking of the things Jules had said. Maybe Tucker would come back, but she wasn't going to count on it. There was no reason to set herself up for disappointment.

She stepped out on the patio to find Tanner there alone. "I guess it's been quite a day for everyone," she said, moving to take a seat on one of the many chairs.

Tanner ran his hand down his face and shook his head. "I don't understand any of it." He looked at Paige and asked, "Are you doing okay?"

"I'm fine," she lied. "And I expect things will get better for all as time goes on."

"I hope so," Tanner replied, as Dusty and Kate, followed by Trish and Morgan, joined them on the patio.

"Where are your little ones?" Paige asked Kate, hoping to take her mind off Tucker.

"Hettie and Aggie wanted to take them for the night," Kate answered. "I just hope they survive."

"I'm sure the babies will do fine," Jules said, joining them.

Kate looked at Trish and grinned. "No, I mean I hope Hettie and Aggie survive."

While everyone laughed, Paige chose to put the events of the day behind her and enjoy herself. Tucker was gone, and it was time to get on with her life with the help of her closest friends, the people now sitting on the patio with her.

"Hey," Dusty said, when Mac and Nikki appeared from around the side of the house, "where's Tucker tonight?"

Tanner looked at Jules, who looked at Paige, who shrugged her shoulders. There wouldn't be any way to keep the news from everyone, so she'd just have to get used to it.

"He left," Tanner answered, glancing at Paige.

Feeling all eyes on her, she simply smiled.

"He'll be back for Shawn's graduation, won't he?" Trish asked.

"Not likely," Tanner admitted, and then began to explain.

"WHERE NEXT? Any idea?"

Tucker looked across the table at Rick and shrugged. This was the second night since he'd left the ranch and he hadn't been able to move on, so he'd returned to Rick's restaurant. "I haven't decided yet."

"I have an extra room, if you need a place to stay," Rick replied. "Until you have some kind of plan."

"Do I need one?" Tucker asked, half serious, half joking.

"It doesn't hurt. I did enough of my own wandering. I even went home and stayed with the family for a while, just like you. But it wasn't until I got serious about my future and took some business classes that things started to come together for me."

"So you didn't just walk in and buy this place."

Rick leaned back in his chair and laughed. "Not even close."

"The business classes helped?"

Grunting, Rick leaned forward again. "Not nearly as much as the shrink did."

Tucker had tried counseling in the VA and it hadn't done any good. And then Jules had suggested it a few times, but he wasn't interested. He didn't think he needed anyone delving into the dark recesses of his mind. He could do that on his own.

"What about your family?" he asked. "Are you in touch with them?"

Rick grinned. "Constantly. At least one of them calls

me every day. But keep in mind that I have five younger brothers and sisters, parents and stepparents and a set of grandparents. Before I went into the service, we were all pretty close. It was only after…"

Tucker knew. He'd heard about what had happened to Rick in Baghdad and knew that it was a miracle the man was sitting across the table from him.

"My stepdad was in Vietnam," Rick continued. "He helped me more than anybody did and encouraged me to see a professional. But it wasn't like it was overnight or anything. You gotta stick with it. And the people around you need to understand. My fiancée left me. She couldn't take it. But I didn't give up. Which reminds me, is there anything going on between you and the lady you brought in here the other night?"

Tucker shook his head, the lump in his throat making it impossible to answer.

"Too bad," Rick said, with a sigh. "She seemed like a real nice lady."

"She's a doctor," Tucker managed to say.

"Yeah?"

Tucker nodded.

After a long whistle, Rick laughed. "They sure don't make 'em like they used to."

Tucker laughed, too, and felt a little better for talking to Rick. Pushing away from the table, he took out his wallet and opened it to pull out some bills. "I'd better call it a night."

Rick reached across the table and stopped him. "This one's on me, buddy. And if you need anything, even if it's only a place to sleep or a friend to talk to, let me know. I'm only a phone call away. I gave you my number the other night, right?"

"Yeah, I have it," Tucker replied, and returned his wallet. "Thanks."

As they both stood, Rick laid a hand on Tucker's shoulder. "That's what friends are for."

"I'll keep in touch," Tucker said, knowing he probably wouldn't.

As he walked toward the door, Rick called out to him. "Next time that doctor shows up, bring her by again."

Tucker nodded and smiled, but he didn't feel even close to happy. Instead of driving directly back to the hotel room he'd gotten the day before, after he'd left Desperation, he drove around Edmond for an hour or so, not caring where he went or what he saw.

Finally returning to his hotel room, he turned on the television, lay back on the bed and hoped he'd soon find respite in sleep.

He didn't.

He was on edge. Nervous. Feeling unbalanced. And he didn't know why.

Or did he?

Hearing the muted sound of thunder outside, he blamed his internal strain on what he guessed was an approaching spring storm. He tried to ignore the tension, just as he'd done at the ranch. When it hadn't worked, he'd taken it as a sign that he needed to leave, hopefully to find a little peace somewhere down the road.

And now he was here, in a hotel room a second night, by himself and with no plans of where he would go next. Drifting, he'd found when he left home to rodeo, wasn't something he dealt with well. The Marine Corps gave him the direction he needed in his life. But now he had nothing and nowhere to go. And if he was completely honest with himself, no one to care about. That was his choice, he knew. Had this one been a bad choice, too?

His mind battled with the ache in his heart. He'd been trying to deny that ache for two days, but it wouldn't go away. He kept telling himself that leaving was the right thing to do, not only for him, but also for his family and, yes, especially for Paige. Leaving might not have been the best choice when he was fifteen, but he was older now and understood more.

Didn't he?

Once again he heard the thunder, and he moved from the bed to stare out the window. Within minutes, huge drops of rain hit the glass and slid down in a trail of moisture, until the window was a distorted blur.

Was this what he wanted? A life of being alone? What would he do? He wasn't fit for the marines now, not unless he wanted a desk job. He didn't. At least he knew that. But what?

There were no answers, not here in this room, for sure. Grabbing a jacket from his duffel, he picked up his room card and left.

The elevator took him down to the lobby, and he felt the urge for some coffee. But the coffee shop was closed, so he went to the lobby desk.

"May I help you, sir?" the young man asked.

"Is there anything open nearby where I can get a cup of coffee at this hour?"

"Yes, sir, there's an all-night diner just up the street."

"Which way?"

The young man pointed, and Tucker thanked him. But at the door, he turned back. "How far is? Within walking distance?"

"Two blocks. But, you might want to drive, considering how hard it's raining."

Tucker smiled and shook his head. "I'll be fine, but thanks."

When he stepped out of the hotel and turned in the direction of where the desk clerk had pointed, he decided the rain was coming down even harder than he'd expected it to be. Puddles had formed on the sidewalk, and he splashed through them on his way. For a moment, he was reminded of a time when he was small, and his mother had taken him and Tanner shopping for summer clothes. He must have been close to four, because it wasn't long before Sally had left. He remembered it had rained, but she hadn't scolded them for getting wet in the puddles. In fact, she'd splashed and laughed along with them.

Sally was expected to be at Shawn's graduation on Tuesday, and Tucker wasn't sure how he felt about that. Tanner had told him he'd felt the same, at first, but had decided it was time to meet her and put the past behind them. Maybe it was, but now that he'd left, Tucker wouldn't be doing that.

He did the best he could to ignore the thoughts and questions that beat at his mind, as he continued on his way to the diner. From a distance, he could see the bright sign, proclaiming the coffee was hot and the pie was delicious, and he quickened his step.

Finally inside and out of the rain, he found an empty booth in the back and started for it, but was brought up short when he saw a woman with dark, curly hair sliding out of one of the booths. When she turned his way, he could see it wasn't Paige, and he realized he'd been holding his breath. Shaking his head at his foolishness, he continued on and finally slid into a booth in the back.

He ordered black coffee and a slice of apple pie from the waitress, then sat back to watch the customers. It was a trick he'd used when he was young and on the road and feeling at loose ends, when his mind warred between doing what he wanted and doing what he should. That war was still going on.

Moving on was the right thing to do, he was sure. His family didn't need him. His son was grown and moving on with his own life. Tucker felt bad about all the pain he'd cause them, over the years. Coming back had only reopened the wounds.

As for Paige, he'd known that he wasn't a man who had the staying power needed to keep a relationship going. Either he ended it or the woman did, and they both went their separate ways. It was better that he move on now, before there were hard feelings between them. Love wasn't something he did well.

And if he just kept telling himself that, everything would be okay.

By the time he made it back to the hotel, the storm had passed on and the sky was beginning to lighten in the east. He tried to sleep, knowing he had a long drive ahead—a drive to nowhere in particular—but he tossed and turned, instead.

The sun was shining brightly when he stuffed his duffel in the back of his vehicle and climbed in behind the wheel, ready to put some miles between him and the recent past. His intention was to head north, toward Kansas, but as he neared the entrance to the interstate highway, he couldn't move his foot from the brake to the accelerator. A car behind him honked, and he stuck his arm out the window to wave the driver around.

It wasn't right. Deep down, he'd known all along that leaving was the wrong thing to do, but he was determined to do it. Only he couldn't. Not now. Maybe not ever.

But if he was going to go home to stay, there were things that needed to be done. After they were and before he saw his family, he was going to tell Paige everything.

Chapter Twelve

Mondays were the worst, Paige decided, as she started her drive home from the clinic at the end of the day. In addition to patient spillovers from the week before, everyone who had put off coming in, hoping they'd feel better, along with those who'd become ill over the weekend were begging for appointments. It was her job to do her best to see them all. Rarely did a Monday go by that she didn't leave the clinic exhausted.

Maybe, she thought, it was time to start looking for a partner—either another doctor or a physician's assistant or nurse practitioner—to help share the ever-growing load of patient care. If she didn't do something soon, she'd be too overworked to help her patients or she could experience burnout. The thought of either happening saddened her as she turned the corner of her street. Her sigh became a gasp when she saw a dark SUV in her driveway.

What was Tucker doing back in Desperation? And why was he at her house?

Her first instinct was to slam on the brakes and hightail it out of there before he had a chance to see her. But she couldn't lift her foot from the accelerator to do it. Her second thought was to keep driving, past her house, around the next corner and out of town, if needed. She didn't want to talk to him. It had taken all of the weekend to get her emotions under control as it was.

Neither happened, and when she approached her driveway, she slowed down and turned in, as she always did. Only this time her heart was racing like a thoroughbred waiting in the gate at Churchill Downs.

Tucker, leaning against the passenger side of his vehicle, raised his hand in greeting. Heart still pounding, Paige opened her car door and slid out.

"I thought you left Desperation." She hadn't meant to sound so accusing, but that's the way it came out.

Tucker's smile was slow as he shrugged. "Let's just say I had second thoughts."

Paige's heart continued to clippity-clop. "How nice for your family." She didn't sound the least bit friendly, even to her own ears, but she chalked that up to not *feeling* friendly. Not after the cold brush-off he'd given her just days before.

He pushed away from the side of the SUV and opened the passenger door. "Get in."

Was he crazy? Had he completely lost his mind? She didn't even bother to answer as she turned and started for the house.

"Paige?"

Not meaning to, she looked back over her shoulder as she started up the porch steps. Even from that far away she could see fear in his eyes and a hint of insecurity. She couldn't ignore him. Her heart wouldn't let her. Her self-preservation, however, was a different story. "What do you want, Tucker?" she asked, regretting the impatience in her voice.

"I—" He stopped and cleared his throat. "I'd like to talk to you."

"About what?"

"I'd like to tell you something."

A million responses popped into her mind, most of them insensitive, but she settled on one that wouldn't hurt quite so much. "I'm listening."

He glanced around as if looking for someone. "Well, it's kind of…"

She waited, wondering how he was going to manage to hurt her again, and then scolded herself for thinking that. "I'm sorry, Tucker, but I'm not going anywhere with you, nor will I get in your SUV or ask you into my home. If you have something to say, you'll just have to say it."

He hesitated for a moment, before nodding. "Okay. I guess I can't blame you for feeling that way."

There was nothing she could say, so she remained silent, waiting.

Stepping away from the SUV, he moved in her direction, but he stopped after only a few steps. "I've never told anyone the things I'm going to tell you," he said. "Maybe I should have. Maybe I will someday soon." When she nodded, he continued. "I'd just turned eighteen when I decided to join the Marine Corps. I thought it would be easy, but they wanted high school graduates, and I'd never finished high school. I went to my grandmother and asked if she knew a way I could get a diploma, as if she had some kind of magic or kept a few up her sleeve, just in case." When she didn't smile, he shrugged and continued. "She sent me to her friend, the head of a school in Tahlequah, who put me through three days of intense testing. When we finished, I'd earned a high school diploma and was eligible to serve my country, as they say."

"Why not a GED?"

"Because I wanted a real diploma from a real school. And I earned every drop of ink on it."

His pride was palpable, and Paige tried not to smile. Tucker had obviously been as stubborn then as he was now. "So you joined the marines."

"Don't let anyone tell you it's easy. I know guys who couldn't make it through boot camp. Of those who did, there were a few who sustained injuries early on, before we ever saw combat." He shrugged and looked past her, as if seeing it all in the distance. "I'd been in for about seven years when I decided to try to get into Special Forces training. When I was finally selected—and it's not something just anybody would want to do—I worked hard. I liked being a marine, maybe because of the structure and discipline." Then something came over his face as he said, "I thought everything was good, until…"

"What happened, Tucker?" she asked in a whisper. Her anger was gone, and even her hurt didn't matter at the moment. He would either tell her this or he wouldn't. It wasn't nearly as important that she know as it was for him to put into words and then let go of.

"I don't know," he answered, still staring off at the early evening sky. "It was a rescue mission, like others we'd done. Five of us were dropped into an area deemed safe enough to get the chopper in and out of, and we, along with the aid workers we were to free, were to meet it at another location."

"And the workers were rescued?"

He nodded, but deep frown lines appeared between

his eyes. "That went fine. We made it to the pick-up point, and then—" He shook his head this time, his breathing quickening. "I don't know. Shots were fired at us, but we managed to get the hostages onto the helicopter, and three of our guys made it on behind them. I remember holding on to the edge of the chopper, Smithson beside me as we lifted off. He took two shots from the rebels, and when I reached out to grab him to keep him from falling, my hand slipped from the helicopter. We hit the ground in a heap, and I guess that's where my knee twisted."

"The helicopter couldn't wait?"

"Not with all the enemy fire. By that time there were dozens of rebels. The mission was to rescue the aid workers, whatever it took. Smithson and I tried to find a safe place to wait it out." His laugh was dry and completely humorless. "We were in an area where there were some mountains and were able to find a place to hide. I did what I could for Smithson's wounds, but it wasn't long before they found us. At one point, I tried to run, but I was run down. That's when my leg was crushed. I guess I was lucky that's all it was."

She'd read the medical report from the VA, so very little of this was new to her. At some point after he'd been rescued, he must have told someone what had happened. "You spent how much time as a prisoner?"

"Nearly nine months."

"And your wounds weren't treated?"

"No. They put us in a cell, if that's what you want to call it, fed us once a day, although most people wouldn't call what we ate food, and that was it. Except for asking questions we had no answers to."

"And Smithson?"

Tucker stopped looking at that faraway point he'd found, and he stared at the ground. "He didn't last a month. They refused to treat his gunshot wounds." For a moment, he was silent. "It was probably a blessing he didn't. I don't know if he could've been saved, even if we'd been found immediately."

"It wasn't your fault, Tucker."

He turned to look at her. "My mind has always told me that, but my heart—" He shook his head.

Understanding that she wasn't trained to give him the help he needed, she moved on. "But you were eventually rescued. How?"

"I don't know. There was this girl... If it hadn't been for her, I might never have lived long enough to have been rescued."

"How old was she?" Paige asked.

"Twelve, maybe? I don't know. She brought the food and water each day, but she would sometimes sneak in late at night and bring extra. She even tried to clean off some of the mud and— I don't know if she had anything to do with my rescue, but it's possible, I guess. She disappeared a few weeks before that."

"So you don't know what happened to her?"

He pressed his lips together and shook his head. "I asked when they picked me up, but no one knew anything. After that, I didn't ask again. I just have a feeling..."

Paige didn't want to go any further with the story. She'd heard all she needed and understood a part of why he was the way he was. Counseling would help, she knew, but she also knew Tucker wasn't interested in giving it a try.

"Thank you for telling me," she said. "I can imagine how difficult it is for you to talk about it."

"I wanted you to know."

He was watching her closely now, as if pinning her to the spot. Her heart had ceased its rapid racing while he told his story, but once again it was back up to speeding along.

"There's just one more thing," he said.

Swallowing was difficult. "What's that?"

"If you'll get in," he said, moving to his vehicle and opening the door, "I'll show you."

She was afraid. She had enough hurt in the past few days and didn't think she could handle any more. "Can't we just—"

"No." His sigh was deep and his voice strained with emotion. "Please, Paige. This is important to me."

How could she deny him? She hadn't stopped loving him, no matter how much she'd told herself it was useless. "All right."

TUCKER WASN'T CONVINCED this was going to work, but he wasn't going to let that stop him. After driving back early that morning from Edmond, he'd been busy. But at least he had something to show for it, and it was Paige he wanted to show it to. She might not be ready to accept what he had to offer, but even if she didn't, he wouldn't give up.

Bringing his SUV to a stop on a road that ran along a little known area at the edge of Desperation, he turned off the engine. Ready to put his plan in action, he stepped out and started around to open the passenger door.

"Where is this?" she asked, climbing out before he could help.

He stopped in front of her when her feet hit the ground. "You don't recognize it?"

"No, I—" She studied the area just off the road, and then looked at him, her head tilted to one side. "The orchard?"

Nodding, he smiled. "What's called the backside."

He shut the door when she stepped away. Shading her eyes with her hands, she checked out their surroundings. "I'm not familiar with this," she admitted. "Help me get my bearings."

"The Commune is over there," he said, pointing ahead and to the left.

"Yes, I think I see it. And the barn, too, I think."

She was standing in front of him, close enough that he could reach out and touch her. And he could smell her perfume. But instead of touching her, he took a step back. "Probably. There's a clearing between here and there. Can you see it?"

"I think so," she answered, sounding doubtful. "Wait! Yes, I see it."

"We used to pitch a tent there, when we were kids," he explained. "We were never allowed to stay overnight, although I never knew why, but there were half a dozen of us, sometimes more, who would stay from early morning until nearly dark, past the time we should've been home."

She turned, looked up at him and smiled. "And you probably all were in trouble."

"I don't remember very many times that we weren't, to be honest." Seeing her standing there, her smile soft and welcoming, it was hard not to touch her, to take her in his arms. But he couldn't. At least not for the time being. He needed to stick to his plan.

When she turned back around, he knew he couldn't wait any longer. "I spent the last couple of days in Edmond," he told her. "In fact, I was headed north, early this morning."

She looked over her shoulder at him. "But you're here."

"I suppose you could say I had an epiphany."

Her eyes widened. "Really?" she said and smiled, as if it was a joke.

"I spent time trying not to think about the things you said to me before I left on Saturday. Not exactly what I'd planned to do, and I never did succeed. And just so you know how close I was to heading north this morning, there were people honking and going around me on the ramp to the interstate."

She'd turned around completely. "So what is it you're saying, Tucker?"

"I'm making some changes in my life," he said simply.

She shook her head. "I guess I don't understand why you're telling me this. You made it clear on Saturday that you were leaving. Has something changed?"

"Lots of things," he said, taking a step closer to her.

But she took a step back. "I'm afraid you'll have to explain, Tucker."

Taking a deep breath, he nodded, realizing she didn't know where he was coming from. He'd blindsided her on Saturday. She'd expected him to stay for Shawn's graduation, and instead, he'd told her he was taking off for parts unknown.

"I talked to Jules early this morning," he said. When she nodded, but said nothing, he continued. "She's found me a therapist at the VA who can help me deal with not only my experiences in Somalia, but my childhood and all the rest. I start seeing him on Thursday."

Her smile was soft and he could almost feel her relief. "That's good, Tucker. Are you moving to Oklahoma City to be closer to the VA?"

He'd had it all planned how he was going to tell her his news, but for some reason, it wasn't coming out the way he'd planned. "No, I'll be staying here."

"At the ranch?"

He shook his head. "Right here. Well, in a few months."

"Here? In Desperation, you mean?"

"That and…well, *here*. Right here."

"I'm afraid I don't understand."

Of course she didn't, and he didn't expect her to. "You see, I need to live in town. For my new job."

"Job?"

He didn't try to hide his smile. "If I pass the exams and the city council approves, I'll be the new sheriff's deputy."

Her brown eyes grew round with surprise. "How—That's—that's wonderful!"

"Thanks go to Morgan for that."

She nodded, but it didn't cover her excitement…or her confusion. "You *have* been busy. I don't know what to say, except…are you sure about all this? I mean, you were so set on leaving, just days ago."

"I was afraid."

"Of what?"

"Pretty much everything, I guess," he answered, not sure what else he could say. But it wasn't the time to explain, even if he could. Pointing to the clearing, he asked, "Can you see the flags?"

"Flags?" she asked, turning around to look.

He laughed when she'd echoed his words again. "Yes. And the strings and stakes."

"Oh! Yes, I can see them."

"The clearing and the land around it is mine. Hettie sold it to me."

"That's fantastic," Paige said.

He looked at the area, and his heart swelled with pride and memories of a happy time. "It took some talking," he admitted. "She really didn't want to sell any of it. It's been in her family for generations. But when I explained what it meant to me, she relented. Not without dragging a promise from me though."

"What kind of promise?" Paige asked.

Tucker was silent for a moment. He wasn't quite ready to tell her. There was more he needed to say, but his old fears were snaking around him. Since he'd turned his SUV around and headed back to Desperation, his courage had grown. Just talking to Jules that morning had forced him to take a hard look at himself, something he'd needed to do for a long time. He hoped that in time he could be the man he should be. Being a loner had suited him when he was younger, but it wasn't what he wanted now. Now he wanted the things he'd never had, never allowed himself to have because he didn't think he deserved them and would ruin anything he got close to. He wanted a family. He wanted love.

That's what he'd realized as he sat at the ramp leading to the interstate, away from the people he cared about and who cared about him. He finally knew that.

"I can't tell you everything Hettie said," he finally

explained. "Not yet, anyway." Sticking his hand in the pocket of his jeans, he pulled out a small, velvet box. "But it involves you."

When he opened the box and held out the emerald-and-diamond ring, she gasped. Looking up at him, he saw that her eyes were glittering with tears. He just wasn't sure if it was happiness or because she was sad. "I've never said this to anyone, but I love you, Paige, and my road to recovery includes you," he told her. "I just don't know how long it'll take me to be the kind of man you deserve."

"Oh, Tucker—"

"You have to be quiet," he said, his voice shaky as he pressed a finger to her lips. "I don't know when my nerve is going to run out here, so let me talk, okay?" When she nodded, he took the ring out of the box and held it. "I was told that emeralds are the symbol of hope, and I guess that's what I have right now." He looked up at her and couldn't read her expression. Not knowing what to think, he ducked his head, ready to say what needed to be said. "I bought it today and planned to ask you to marry me—"

"Tucker—"

"—but then I thought it might be too soon for you to even think about that—"

"If you'd—"

"—so I thought it might be better as a gift of what the future—" He didn't know what was happening when she put her hand over his mouth, but he stopped talking and stared at her.

"Will you hush?" she said, wiping a tear from her cheek. "I love you, Tucker. That's what I've been trying to tell you, but you won't be quiet long enough—" She let out a deep sigh and shook her head, her hand still across his mouth. "For a man who had little to say when we first met, you sure are talking too much right now. But if you just can't be quiet, would you please—"

Tucker gently moved her hand from his mouth. "Paige, will you marry me?"

THE ROCKING O Ranch was lit up like a birthday cake, welcoming family, friends and neighbors, who had come to share in the celebration of Shawn's graduation from high school. The patio at the back of the house was filled with people, and so were the family room and kitchen.

Tucker couldn't remember a time he'd ever felt so proud. His son had not only graduated from high school less than an hour before, but Shawn had also been one of two salutatorians, the other being his best friend, Ryan. It was shaping up to be a surprise-filled night. He and Paige had shared their news with Shawn the night before, but they wanted to wait to tell the others, so Shawn could bask in the limelight before leaving for several other after-graduation parties.

"There you are!"

Tucker turned to discover his sister wearing a wide smile, as she grabbed his arm and tugged. "Where are we going?" he asked.

"You and Tanner are impossible to keep track of," Nikki said, as he allowed her to drag him up the steps and into the house through the double glass patio doors. "The photographer is here and wants to get some family shots."

"Can it wait just a few minutes?" he asked. "There's

someone—" And then he saw Paige, coming out of the kitchen. "I'll be there in a minute," he promised.

Nikki looked up at him, her usually up-turned mouth turned down in a frown. "If I have to come looking for you again—"

"You won't."

With a sigh, Nikki walked away, and he moved to where Paige had stopped to talk to Trish. "Now might be a good time," he told her, when he was able to get her attention for a moment.

She looked at him and smiled, making him wish the evening was over and they could spend some time alone. He knew that wouldn't happen, but it didn't bother him as much as it might other men. His family loved her, and so did most everyone else in Desperation.

Putting his arm around her waist, he eased her away from Trish, whose eyes had grown wide and a smile was slowly forming. "Family photos," he explained, as if that wouldn't raise some questions.

"Can I put it on now?" Paige asked.

"Definitely," he answered.

"I'll have to get my purse. It's in the kitchen."

"I knew I should've kept it," he called to her as she went to retrieve the ring. "Meet me out on the patio, okay?"

"Okay," she answered, with a wave as she disappeared.

He looked down to see Kirby, Mac and Nikki's son, watching him. "I'm supposed to tell you to hurry up."

"Show me where I need to go."

Five minutes later, Tucker stood on one side of the mother who had left them when they were boys, and Tanner stood on the other side of her. "I know how hard this has been for both of you," Sally said, as the photographer adjusted his lens.

"Don't worry about it," Tanner answered. "Nobody in this family is perfect, and it's time to put the past behind us." He leaned in front of her. "Isn't that right, Tucker?"

"Very right," he answered, unable to keep from smiling. He'd thought it would be hard to meet Sally, but the instant he saw her, he was bombarded with happy memories, and it wasn't long before all those years had melted away and they were all talking at once.

The picture was finally snapped, and the photographer looked around. "Are there any more I need to get?"

"Stick around for a few more minutes," Tanner said. He quickly excused himself to Sally, leaving Tucker alone with her.

"None of this has been easy, has it?" she asked him.

Tucker shook his head. "I don't think life is supposed to be."

"I think you're right," she said, just as the sound of an old-fashioned dinner bell started ringing.

"What the—"

Tanner, holding the triangular-shaped metal bell, made his way through the crowd to the steps leading to the house. "Stay right where you are," Tanner said, when Tucker started to move away. "I've heard there's some news you need to share with the family, and I'm sure all our friends would be happy to hear it, too."

Tucker, totally taken by surprise, wasn't sure what to say or do. He was immediately joined by Paige, thanks to some help from Jules and the other ladies.

"Shame on you for keeping secrets, Tucker O'Brien," Jules whispered as she stepped aside.

Paige moved closer to him. "I think we're supposed to make an announcement," she whispered.

"Did you tell them?" he asked. They'd agreed not to tell anyone but Shawn.

"Not a soul," she said. "Not even Garrett or my parents."

"Then who—?"

Tanner, who hadn't moved and stood as if guarding him, in case he might make a run for it, clanged the bell again. "We have some family news to share," he said, in a voice loud enough to be heard in the next county. The crowd quickly quieted, and he continued. "As you all know, my baby brother came home a couple of months ago."

"Baby?" Tucker repeated.

Tanner laughed. "Younger, then," he said, grinning. "We haven't had much time to get reacquainted with each other, and he's still learning the names of new family and friends, but he's coming along. There's one thing we didn't count on, though. While we were worrying about him and wondering if he'd want to stay and be a part of us, he was off finding someone to marry. Friends, please join in celebrating with us the engagement of Tucker O'Brien and Dr. Paige Miles."

Friends and neighbors gathered around to extend not only their surprise, but also their best wishes. Because there'd been no wedding date set yet, and wouldn't be until a finish date on the new house was known, there wasn't a whole lot to tell people. Although Tucker felt totally out of his element, he also felt the love of everyone who spoke to them and wondered why it had taken him so long to return to the Rocking O.

Hours later, when the last of the guests were gone, and Jules had collapsed in the family room, along with Bridey, Nikki and Paige, Tanner and Tucker stood in the backyard, looking at the stars.

"I don't remember ever being this happy," Tucker said, his heart aching with joy.

"There'll be more times," Tanner replied. "You can count on it. You're not too old to be a father again, you know."

Tucker stared at him, not knowing quite how to answer. "I don't know. Paige and I have never talked about it."

"There's no rush."

"That's good," Tucker said with a nervous laugh.

"Ready to go inside?"

With a nod, they turned for the house. Once inside, Tanner went to sit by Jules, moving her closer when he put his arm around her. Tucker walked over to where Paige was sitting and bent down to kiss her.

"It's been quite a night," Paige said, as he sat beside her.

Tucker looked around at everyone, wondering how he could've been so lucky. "Don't ever let me leave, Paige," he whispered to her. "Not ever. Not for any reason. I know now that I belong here, and you belong here with me."

She placed her hand in his, and he laced his fingers with her. He couldn't understand why he'd been blessed, not only with the family he'd left behind, but with a woman as wonderful as her.

Bridey got to her feet. "Anybody hungry?" she asked,

looking around the room. As if they were magic words, everyone jumped up at once.

"The O'Briens are finally complete," Tanner said, as they all walked to the kitchen.

"That we are," Tucker replied, and turned to his bride-to-be. "And so am I."

* * * * *

Return to Desperation in
Roxann Delaney's next book
and find out who captures
Garrett Miles's heart!

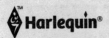 **Harlequin**®

 *American ★ Romance*®

COMING NEXT MONTH

Available July 12, 2011

#1361 THE TEXAN AND THE COWGIRL
American Romance's Men of the West
Victoria Chancellor

#1362 THE COWBOY'S BONUS BABY
Callahan Cowboys
Tina Leonard

#1363 HER COWBOY DADDY
Texas Legacies: The McCabes
Cathy Gillen Thacker

#1364 THE BULL RIDER'S SECRET
Rodeo Rebels
Marin Thomas

You can find more information on upcoming
Harlequin® titles, free excerpts and more at
www.HarlequinInsideRomance.com.

REQUEST YOUR FREE BOOKS!
2 FREE NOVELS PLUS 2 FREE GIFTS!

◆ Harlequin®

American ★ Romance®

LOVE, HOME & HAPPINESS

YES! Please send me 2 FREE Harlequin American Romance® novels and my 2 FREE gifts (gifts are worth about $10). After receiving them, if I don't wish to receive any more books, I can return the shipping statement marked "cancel." If I don't cancel, I will receive 4 brand-new novels every month and be billed just $4.24 per book in the U.S. or $4.99 per book in Canada. That's a saving of at least 15% off the cover price! It's quite a bargain! Shipping and handling is just 50¢ per book in the U.S. and 75¢ per book in Canada.* I understand that accepting the 2 free books and gifts places me under no obligation to buy anything. I can always return a shipment and cancel at any time. Even if I never buy another book, the two free books and gifts are mine to keep forever.

154/354 HDN FDKS

Name	(PLEASE PRINT)	

Address		Apt. #

City	State/Prov.	Zip/Postal Code

Signature (if under 18, a parent or guardian must sign)

Mail to the **Reader Service:**
IN U.S.A.: P.O. Box 1867, Buffalo, NY 14240-1867
IN CANADA: P.O. Box 609, Fort Erie, Ontario L2A 5X3

Not valid for current subscribers to Harlequin American Romance books.

Want to try two free books from another line?
Call 1-800-873-8635 or visit www.ReaderService.com.

* Terms and prices subject to change without notice. Prices do not include applicable taxes. Sales tax applicable in N.Y. Canadian residents will be charged applicable taxes. Offer not valid in Quebec. This offer is limited to one order per household. All orders subject to credit approval. Credit or debit balances in a customer's account(s) may be offset by any other outstanding balance owed by or to the customer. Please allow 4 to 6 weeks for delivery. Offer available while quantities last.

Your Privacy—The Reader Service is committed to protecting your privacy. Our Privacy Policy is available online at www.ReaderService.com or upon request from the Reader Service.

We make a portion of our mailing list available to reputable third parties that offer products we believe may interest you. If you prefer that we not exchange your name with third parties, or if you wish to clarify or modify your communication preferences, please visit us at www.ReaderService.com/consumerschoice or write to us at Reader Service Preference Service, P.O. Box 9062, Buffalo, NY 14269. Include your complete name and address.

HARII

USA TODAY *bestselling author B.J. Daniels
takes you on a trip to Whitehorse, Montana,
and the Chisholm Cattle Company.*

RUSTLED

Available July 2011 from Harlequin Intrigue.

As the dust settled, Dawson got his first good look at the rustler. A pair of big Montana sky-blue eyes glared up at him from a face framed by blond curls.

A woman rustler?

"You have to let me go," she hollered as the roar of the stampeding cattle died off in the distance.

"So you can finish stealing my cattle? I don't think so." Dawson jerked the woman to her feet.

She reached for the gun strapped to her hip hidden under her long barn jacket.

He grabbed the weapon before she could, his eyes narrowing as he assessed her. "How many others are there?" he demanded, grabbing a fistful of her jacket. "I think you'd better start talking before I tear into you."

She tried to fight him off, but he was on to her tricks and pinned her to the ground. He was suddenly aware of the soft curves beneath the jean jacket she wore under her coat.

"You have to listen to me." She ground out the words from between her gritted teeth. "You have to let me go. If you don't they will come back for me and they will kill you. There are too many of them for you to fight off alone. You won't stand a chance and I don't want your blood on my hands."

"I'm touched by your concern for me. Especially after you just tried to pull a gun on me."

"I wasn't going to shoot you."

Dawson hauled her to her feet and walked her the rest of the way to his horse. Reaching into his saddlebag, he pulled out a length of rope.

"You can't tie me up."

He pulled her hands behind her back and began to tie her wrists together.

"If you let me go, I can keep them from coming back," she said. "You have my word." She let out an unladylike curse. "I'm just trying to save your sorry neck."

"And I'm just going after my cattle."

"Don't you mean your boss's cattle?"

"Those cattle are mine."

"*You're* a Chisholm?"

"Dawson Chisholm. And you are…?"

"Everyone calls me Jinx."

He chuckled. "I can see why."

Bronco busting, falling in love…it's all in a day's work.
Look for the rest of their story in

RUSTLED

Available July 2011 from Harlequin Intrigue
wherever books are sold.

Copyright © 2011 by Barbara Heinlein

HIEXP0711R

Love Inspired

After her fiancé calls off their wedding, Brooke Clayton has nowhere to go but home. Turns out the wealthy businessman next door, handsome single father Gabe Wesson, needs a nanny for his toddler—and Brooke needs a job. But Gabe sees Brooke as a reminder of the young wife he lost. Given their pasts, do they dare hope to fit together as a family…forever?

The Nanny's Homecoming
by Linda Goodnight

◀ ROCKY MOUNTAIN HEIRS ▶

Available July wherever books are sold.

www.LoveInspiredBooks.com

LI87680

Harlequin®

SPECIAL EDITION

Life, Love and Family

THE TEXANS ARE COMING!

Reader-favorite miniseries Montana Mavericks
is back in Special Edition with new loves,
adventures and more.

July 2011 features *USA TODAY* bestselling author
CHRISTINE RIMMER
with
RESISTING MR. TALL, DARK & TEXAN.

A Texas oil mogul arrives in Thunder Canyon on
business and soon falls for his personal assistant. Only
one problem—she's just resigned to open a bakery!
Can he convince her to stay on—as his bride?

Find out in July!

Look for a new
Montana Mavericks: The Texans Are Coming **title**
in each of these months

August	September	October
November	December	

Available wherever books are sold.

www.Harlequin.com

SEMM0711

ROMANTIC SUSPENSE

Secrets and scandal ignite in a danger-filled,
passion-fuelled new miniseries.

**Family. Lies.
Full exposure.**

When scandal erupts, threatening California Senator
Hank Kelley's career and his life, there's only one place he can
turn—the family ranch in Maple Cove, Montana. But he'll need
the help of his estranged sons and their friends to pull the family
together despite attempts on his life and pressure from a sinister
secret society, and to prevent an unthinkable tragedy that would
shake the country to its core.

Collect all 6 heart-racing tales starting July 2011 with

Private Justice

by *USA TODAY* bestselling author

MARIE FERRARELLA

Special Ops Bodyguard by **BETH CORNELISON** (August 2011)

Cowboy Under Siege by **GAIL BARRETT** (September 2011)

Rancher Under Cover by **CARLA CASSIDY** (October 2011)

Missing Mother-To-Be by **ELLE KENNEDY** (November 2011)

Captain's Call of Duty by **CINDY DEES** (December 2011)

www.Harlequin.com

HRS27734

Looking for a great Western read?

We have just the thing!

A Cowboy for Every Mood

Visit
www.HarlequinInsideRomance.com
for a sneak peek and exciting exclusives
on your favorite cowboy heroes.

Pick up next month's cowboy books
by some of your favorite authors:

Vicki Lewis Thompson
Carla Cassidy
B.J. Daniels
Rachel Lee
Christine Rimmer
Donna Alward
Cheryl St.John
And many more…

Available wherever books are sold.

ACFEM0611R